A KIND OF THIEF

Also by Vivien Alcock

A KIND OF THIEF

Vivien Alcock

Delacorte Press

Published by
Delacorte Press
Bantam Doubleday Dell Publishing Group, Inc.
666 Fifth Avenue
New York, New York 10103

This edition was first published in Great Britain
in 1991 by Methuen Children's Books,
a division of the Octopus Publishing Group

Library of Congress Cataloging in Publication Data
Alcock, Vivien.
A kind of thief / Vivien Alcock.
p. cm.
Summary: When her father is suddenly arrested and put into prison,
thirteen-year-old Elinor finds that she has to face many unpleasant truths
about him and their way of life.
ISBN 0-385-30564-8
[1. Fathers—Fiction. 2. Family problems—Fiction. 3. Prisoners—Fiction.
4. Interpersonal relations—Fiction.] I. Title.
PZ7.A334Ki 1992
[Fic]—dc20   91-25556
                                                                        CIP
                                                                         AC

Manufactured in the United States of America

February 1992

10 9 8 7 6 5 4 3 2 1

BVG

To Sheila and Eric

Contents

Chapter One

THEY CAME early, ringing at the bell, knocking at the door, and shouting. Elinor's room was at the back of the house. The noise disturbed her dreams, and she pulled her quilt over her head. Unlike her sister Judy, she was bad at waking up. It took her a long time to clear her mind of sleep.

The sound of Bambi crying finally roused her. He had a loud voice. Her young stepmother, Sophia, claimed he'd be a famous opera singer one day. Maybe. If he lived that long. Why didn't Sophia get up and feed him, the lazy pig? Elinor got out of bed, put on her dressing gown, and opened the door of her room.

Something was wrong!

The light was on in the hall below, and she could hear Sophia's voice raised in an angry wail, the words so muddled with tears that it was impossible to tell whether she was speaking in English or Italian. Then a man said something Elinor could not hear. She ran to the banister and looked down into the hall.

Sophia was there, in her white woolen dressing gown, clutching Bambi so tightly and jiggling him up and down

1

in such a rough and nervous manner that it was no wonder he was crying, poor baby.

Judy was crying, too, her face red and streaked with tears, her nightdress creased and her feet bare. Their father, however, was dressed in a dark gray suit, his thick hair well brushed, his tie neatly tied, and his shoes polished. Only his face was crumpled and uncertain as if, for the first time, he didn't know what to do. When he saw Elinor coming down the stairs, he looked relieved.

"Here's Elinor," he said, almost as if he expected her to put everything right.

But Elinor had no idea what to do or what was happening. Judy ran over to her and clung to her arm, crying.

"Don't let them! Don't let them, Ellie!"

"Don't let who what?" she asked, bewildered and afraid.

There were two strange men in the hall, standing stiffly by the door. The older one was regarding her gloomily, as if he thought she only added to his troubles. The younger one was watching her father. Somehow they frightened her, coming here before the sun was properly up. She knew at once they meant her family no good.

Pulling away from Judy, she ran over to her father.

"What's happened, Dad? Have they taken us hostage? Who are they? Are they criminals?"

Before her father could answer, her stepmother began laughing hysterically, surprising Bambi so that he stopped screaming on a hiccup, and twisted in her arms to stare at her.

"Criminals? No, no!" she cried, her great dark eyes

looking wild. "They are the police, that is who. They come to take your papa to prison, that is who." She turned on the men and shrieked at them, "You will be sorry. My husband is important man. He knows top people. Georgio, tell them—" The rest of what she was saying was drowned out by Bambi's renewed screams.

"For God's sake, Sophia," George Forest said. "You're frightening the children, not the inspector. If you can't keep Bambi quiet, take him up to his room. Put him in his cot. Feed him or something. Only stop him from making that filthy row!"

Elinor had never heard her father speak so roughly to Sophia before. Her stepmother looked furious, as if she would have hit him but for the baby in her arms. Then her face crumpled and she turned and ran up the stairs.

"I spit on you!" she screamed down from the top, but whether this was intended for her husband or the policemen was not certain. She turned away, a door slammed, and the baby's screams were muted.

The older man said something to her father Elinor could not hear. She saw her father nod. Then he came over to her and said, "Elinor, I have to go to the police station with the inspector to sort one or two things out—"

"What things? What's happened? Why have you got to go?"

"Oh . . . it's a business matter. I haven't time to explain now. Sophia will tell you later. Be a good girl."

"I don't believe they're policemen," Judy said. She had stopped crying and was staring at the men suspiciously.

"Judy, please—"

"If they're policemen, why aren't they in uniform?" she demanded.

"Because they're in plain clothes."

"Anyone could say that," Judy said, looking stubborn.

"That's enough, Judy," her father said, controlling his voice with an effort. "Elinor, take her into the living room—"

"No! I won't go!" the little girl cried, dodging away before Elinor could move. "I won't!" Her mouth became a wobbly oblong, as it always did before she cried.

"Show us your arrest warrant," Elinor said, supporting her sister as she always did. "Go on."

"Where's that girl gone, what's-her-name?" the inspector said to his companion irritably. "Why isn't she here? She should be dealing with this."

"You sent her out to the car, sir."

"She's taking her time coming back."

"Show me your warrant! I want to see your warrant!" Judy cried. "Show me!"

"Judy!" her father said, then shrugged and turned to the policemen. "You brought this on yourselves," he told the men. "Why couldn't you have come to my office, instead of here, in front of my children."

"We did go to your office," the younger man said. Elinor hated him, with his sleek fair hair and his eyes as bright as pins. "We were told you hadn't been there for weeks."

"You could have telephoned me. Was it necessary to come bursting in in the middle of the night? Frightening my wife—"

"It's five in the morning," the inspector said, "and we were just in time, weren't we, sir? I notice you are already up and dressed. Were you thinking of making a journey? To South America, perhaps?"

"No!" their father shouted.

"Is that your suitcase over there?" the inspector asked, pointing.

Elinor and Judy stared across the hall to where a brown case was standing by the wall, then back at their father. His face was red and he didn't answer.

"No! It isn't his! It's mine!" Judy cried. She ran over and sat on it, staring up at the policemen defiantly. "It's mine. I put it there. I'm going to the seaside."

For the first time since they'd come, both men looked away from George Forest at the same time. On an impulse he took something out of his pocket, put his arm around Elinor, and hugged her, whispering something she couldn't hear. To her astonishment she felt his hand slip in and out of her dressing-gown pocket so quickly that she almost thought she'd imagined it. She felt her cheeks flush.

"Don't *you* cry, Elinor," he said, his hand tightening warningly on her arm, "I'm counting on you. You're the strong one in the family, the sensible one. Look after them for me, won't you?"

Elinor didn't answer. She felt stupid with surprise. The inspector was looking at her.

He must notice how red my face is, she thought, her heart thumping, I must look guilty. I feel guilty, though I haven't done anything.

She'd never been frightened of the police before. They were the protectors. They helped children and old ladies across the street and kept an eye on your house at night. They couldn't be arresting Dad. He wasn't the sort of man who got arrested. Everybody admired and respected him, she knew they did. People had said to her, "What a charming man your father is." She'd been proud of him. It must be a mistake. Sophia must've got it wrong. Sophia often got things wrong. It came of being Italian and not understanding English properly. . . .

Her father was talking to her.

"What?" she asked, confused. A policewoman had just come in the front door and the inspector was saying something to her in a low voice.

"Do pay attention, Elinor," her father said. "Remind Sophia to ring Walter—"

"Who?"

"Walter. Walter Brimly. My lawyer. She'll know. Goodbye, my dear."

"Dad—"

"Now, Ellie, no tears," he said, smiling at her. It was too late to say this to Judy, who was crying again and clinging to him with both hands. He kissed her and thrust her into Elinor's arms. Then he joined the detectives. They opened the front door and Elinor saw more policemen in uniform outside and police cars by the curb.

"Dad—"

She tried to run out after him, but the policewoman stepped forward and blocked her way, saying something she didn't listen to. Sophia came running down the stairs, pushed past them all, and ran down to the gate. But the car had already started. Judy pulled away from Elinor and ran to her, and she knelt down and hugged her, both of them crying.

"What about putting the kettle on and making everyone a nice cup of tea?" the policewoman said to Elinor.

Elinor turned without a word and went to the kitchen. It was quiet in there. The policewoman did not follow her. She put her hand into her dressing-gown pocket and took out a small piece of paper. It was a buff-colored oblong, about two by four inches. At the top was printed in black: VICTORIA B.R. The smaller print underneath was almost obliterated by a large oval date stamp 2 March 1992. She stared at it, realizing what it was. Three days ago, for it was now 5 March, her father had deposited something at the baggage check at Victoria Station.

A sudden noise made her start guiltily and she thrust the ticket back into her pocket. But it was only Sophia and Judy coming back.

Chapter Two

ELINOR DID not tell Sophia about the baggage receipt. If Dad had wanted Sophia to have it, he'd have given it to her. Stood to reason. No. He'd meant Elinor to have it. He'd chosen her to trust. "You're the strong one in the family," he'd said. "The sensible one."

Was she? She didn't feel it. She was only thirteen.

But someone had to take charge. Her stepmother was so erratic, always up and down, now singing like a bird, now wailing like a trodden-on cat. And her temper! Elinor had seen her shake little Bambi once till she'd thought his head would fly off. The next moment Sophia had been all tears and kisses.

"You shouldn't have done that," Elinor had said, shocked. "You could've hurt him."

"I know. I am a pig." Sophia had wept. "I didn't mean to. My poor little baby, I didn't mean to!" And she'd cried so much that Elinor had had to comfort her.

You couldn't dislike Sophia. Nobody could. But you couldn't depend on her.

She'd come into their lives nearly two years ago,

8

walking in out of the summer rain, while their father, back from a business trip in Italy, was paying off the taxi.

"Who's she?" Judy had asked, in what was intended to be a whisper but had come out too loud. The young woman had heard her and laughed.

"I'm your new mama," she'd said, kneeling down and taking Judy into her arms. "We will be friends, yes?"

Judy, who was only five then, had been confused. The woman was soft and very pretty, with auburn hair and glossy black eyes, and she smelled nice. But Judy wasn't certain whether she ought to let people she didn't know hug her, and she looked over the woman's shoulder to see how her brother and sister were taking it.

Matthew, dazzled by the woman's bright eyes and quick voice and the flashing diamonds on her fingers, stood and stared.

Elinor was furious.

"Dad, you haven't married her, have you?" she whispered when her father came in, adding quickly when she saw him look angry, "I mean, she's too young."

"She's nineteen," her father said crossly. "Not that it's any of your business. You talk as if I'm an old man. Well, I'm not." He glanced over at the others, who were chattering and laughing now, and went on, "Ellie, don't make things difficult for me. I told you I'd probably get married again one day and you were very sweet about it. Very understanding."

"Yes, but that was different," Elinor said.

Their mother had died when Judy was only a baby and Matthew so young that Elinor wondered if he could remember her. Even her own memories, though she treasured them, were becoming dim. She could not really blame Dad for wanting to marry again, but she hadn't expected it to happen until they'd grown up and left home. She hadn't actually thought of a stepmother, merely a new wife for Dad, who'd been a widower for so long. And she certainly hadn't expected an Italian girl, as pretty as paint, with her skirts too short and her heels too high. A mother? Her? No!

"She's only eight years older than me. She can't possibly be my mother."

The young woman had sharp ears. She turned around and smiled at Elinor.

"I can be a stepmother. You can be stepmother though very young. In Napoli where I live, we know a woman who have stepmother more young than she." She made a comic face and added, "She is a leetle cross at first but now they are like sisters." Getting to her feet, she came over. "You are Elinor, yes? Your papa tell me good things about you. I think I am disappointment to you? You like stepmother to be old and fat?"

Elinor could not help laughing with her. She was so very pretty. And she had brought them fascinating presents from Italy: little gilded horses, glass birds, silk scarves, and straw hats for Elinor and Judy, and a painted carnival mask like a great bird's head for Matthew.

"Your papa pay for them because I have no money," she'd said, laughing. "But me, I think of it. I choose."

Yes, it was difficult to dislike Sophia.

Though I could manage it quite easily now, Elinor thought, remembering the scene there had been when Sophia and Judy had come in from watching the police car drive away to find there were still policemen in the house.

"Get out! Get out, all of you!" Sophia had screamed at them. "What are you doing? You have taken my husband, is that not enough? What you want now? You want to arrest this little girl?" she'd demanded, offering them Judy, who'd promptly burst into tears. "Or my little baby?"

"Sophia, they've got a search warrant," Elinor had said, her face crimson with embarrassment.

"Search warrant? I do not believe. Where? Show it to me," Sophia had demanded, and on being shown the warrant, had torn it into two and burst into tears. And Elinor had wished with all her heart that her father had married an older, more sensible woman. Like the vicar's wife. Or Miss Bailey at school.

The house was quiet now. The police had gone at last. They had searched the house, but not the people in it. The baggage receipt was still safe in Elinor's dressing-gown pocket.

"Judy, we have cried enough," Sophia was saying. They were all in the kitchen, still in their nightclothes, having coffee and toast. "Here is Elinor with her eyes dry, being an example to us."

"Ellie never cries. She can't. She's a freak," Judy said, sniffing. "I bet Matthew cries."

Their brother had spent the night with a friend and wasn't due back until lunchtime. Elinor glanced at the kitchen clock and was amazed to find it was only a quarter past ten. She felt as though the police had been in their house for days.

"What will you tell Matthew, Sophia?" she asked.

Her stepmother shrugged and spread her hands. "What can I tell him, poor boy. I tell him his papa is in prison—"

"Not prison," Elinor interrupted. "The police station."

"Prison, police station, it is all the same. They put him in the cell and lock the door. No, no more crying now, Judy. You blow your nose and then do me a big favor. You go upstairs and dress yourself, very quiet so you don't wake Bambi, yes? Then you go next door and ask Mrs. Crabbe if she let you have some sugar. Tell her we run out."

When Judy had left the room, Elinor said, "She'll tell them about Dad. You know she will. She can never keep things to herself. The whole street will know."

"It does not matter. Who cares? You think they don't look out of their windows when the police come, making noise to wake the dead? I think Mrs. Crabbe come any minute to borrow something. We get in first and have a little peace."

Elinor was silent for a moment, then she asked, "What's Dad supposed to have done? They must've said when they arrested him."

Her stepmother pushed her hair back from her face. "Oh, I forget," she said. "Something—what was it? Something like stealing by false accounting, obtaining property by deception . . . I don't know, they went on and on."

"Stealing?"

"I think they say stealing. I don't remember. It is about money. It is always about money. Your papa do something he should not in business."

"You mean you think he's guilty?"

"No, no. I do not think. How should I know? Your

papa tell me nothing. I know he want to be rich. Everybody want to be rich. It is natural. He does something a little foolish, perhaps. But he will explain and everything will be all right. You see."

She looked at Elinor with her great dark eyes and Elinor knew that she was frightened too.

They were silent for a moment. Then Elinor said, "Why don't you try Walter Brimly again? He should be in by now."

"That man," Sophia said. "I do not trust him."

"But he's Dad's lawyer. He's been here to dinner."

"I know that. I cook the dinner. I don't like him. He is greedy like the pig. I think he talk your papa into it, whatever it is. I think he's already gone like the others."

"What others?"

"The other fat men. Your papa's business partners. They come to dinner, too, but now they have run off and left my poor Georgio to face the soup."

"*Music,* face the music," Elinor said. "Where have they gone?"

Sophia shrugged. "They do not tell me. Somewhere far away and hot, with no extradition treaty. Maybe hell," she said thoughtfully. She shivered and looked through the window at the daffodils shaking in the windy garden. "Why is it always cold here?" she asked, and began to cry.

Above their heads Bambi started howling, as if in sympathy.

Chapter Three

ELINOR KEPT going to the window and looking out, hoping to see her brother coming. At first she had been buoyed up by a sense of unreality. The arrest of her father had seemed like a film in which she had a part to play. Soon the director would say, "Cut!" and everyone would relax and have coffee and doughnuts. But nobody said "cut"—it just went on and on. When Sophia went out, and Elinor was alone in the house except for Bambi asleep upstairs, she felt frightened.

Matthew came home just before one, his hair still damp and ruffled from swimming. He was a thin, excitable boy. When Elinor told him their father had been arrested, he went as white as his shirt.

"He's killed someone, hasn't he? He drives too fast. He nearly hit a dog the other day. It ran out—"

"It's nothing to do with a dog. It's money. He's stolen—"

"Dad wouldn't steal," he said flatly. "You're joking, I suppose. It's a pretty stupid joke, if you ask me. Where's Sophia?"

"She's gone to the police station with some stuff for

Dad," she told Matthew. "He's got to stay the night there. It isn't a joke, Matt. Dad's been arrested for—um—false accounting and obtaining money by deception. That's what Sophia told me."

"Dad wouldn't cheat either," Matthew said with perfect faith.

Elinor wished she could still feel as certain. Like Matthew, she'd taken Dad's honesty for granted. Now she couldn't forget his furtive hand slipping the luggage receipt into her pocket, and the urgent whisper she hadn't heard, but knew she mustn't ask him to repeat, not with the police there. She felt he was no longer the father she'd thought him to be and she was frightened.

"She's meeting the lawyer there," she went on. "I wanted to go with her but she wouldn't let me. She said to tell you not to come either. We'd only be in the way and they wouldn't let us see Dad. We'd just have to sit in a drafty corridor, getting under everyone's feet."

"She seems to know a lot about police stations, doesn't she?" Matthew said. "Where's Judy?"

"Having lunch next door. Mrs. Crabbe said to bring you over and she'd give us all lunch but I said you'd be tired. You didn't want to go, did you?"

"No!"

"Sophia left us sandwiches. Come into the kitchen and I'll make you hot chocolate," she offered, for he looked pale and cold.

Once in the kitchen, she felt more cheerful. The sun was shining through the window, patterning the table with yellow lozenges, and the smell of fresh brown bread was comforting. Matthew kept asking her questions—

what exactly had Sophia said? What had the police said?
What had Dad said? Where had they searched?

"Not my room!" he cried.

"Everywhere."

"Did they—did they find anything?"

"I don't think so. They didn't say."

"I wish I'd been there," he said. "I wish I hadn't
missed it. Ellie, have you told me everything? You're not
keeping something back, are you?"

"No," she said. The baggage ticket, now folded into a
neat square, was strapped to her chest with two strips of
surgical tape, just in case the police came back to search
again. She wondered whether to tell him about it. She
longed to tell someone.

Matthew was only nine but she knew she could trust
him to keep quiet. He was a naturally secretive boy. He
never chattered about his friends or told them what happened at school, and he kept his diary hidden beneath a
loose floorboard in his room. Elinor knew this because
she had found it there. When Matthew was small, he had
often taken her things and hidden them, and she'd got
into the habit of searching his room whenever she lost
anything. Though he must have noticed that she'd taken
her things back, he had never changed his hiding place,
and his diary, which she'd once opened, contained nothing more revealing than—Monday—Tea with Peter. Tuesday—Dentist. Wednesday—Violin lesson. He was a funny
boy. Not that he'd pinched anything for years, but you
never knew.

Takes after Dad, I suppose, she thought.

"What will happen now?" he asked.

"Dad's to come before the magistrates tomorrow

morning, and they'll decide—I dunno—I suppose whether there's enough evidence to go on."

"There won't be. They'll let him go. They'll see at once he isn't the sort of man who'd steal. He wouldn't! He wouldn't ever! He's terribly strict about"—his eyes shifted away from hers—"about things like that. I mean, he's all for law and order. He won't even park on a yellow line."

But he drives too fast, Elinor thought.

Sophia was not out for long. She came back in a rush, her chestnut hair all tangled by the wind, her cheeks flushed. She hugged them both, told them their father sent his love and they were not to worry, and then rushed upstairs to see Bambi.

"He is the lucky one," she told Elinor, who had followed her up. "Look how he is sleeping, so good and fat. He knows where his next meal is coming from. Me. He doesn't worry that we will soon be in the street. He think it will last forever."

"In the street?"

"Ssh, don't wake him. There is no money, nothing left. It all belong to the company, the house, the car. They throw us in the road—" she cried, her English slipping wildly, as it always did when she was excited. Then, seeing Elinor's frightened face, she said quickly, "But don't worry. Walter Brimly will tell us what to do. I think I am wrong about him. Perhaps he is a good lawyer. At least he has not run away like the others. He say your papa is unfortunate."

"Unfortunate?"

"I think he mean he is too honest to make a good

criminal," Sophia said bitterly. "I didn't know I am marrying a criminal. It is not what I choose. But if I have to, I wish him to be a good criminal, who think about his family and has a secret bank account in Switzerland—" Her face changed and she turned to Elinor eagerly. "But perhaps I am wrong. He say you have something for me. A receipt, no?"

"A receipt?" Elinor asked, and felt herself flushing. So he had not trusted her. He'd only used her pocket because Sophia had gone upstairs. She was just to be a mailbox between them.

"I think he say a receipt," her stepmother went on, frowning. "It is difficult. They do not leave us alone. There is always someone, the police, the lawyer. He has to whisper in Italian when he kiss me good-bye. They do not like that, but he says he is only telling me he love me." Sophia smiled as if she thought that had been amazingly clever. "But what he really say is, 'Ask Elinor for the receipt. She'll know.' Then he say in English, 'Look after them for me, darling, all my little ones.' "

He asked *me* to, Elinor thought bitterly, all her old jealousy flaring up. He said I was the strong one of the family. He asked me to look after everything. Why did he have to tell Sophia? They are my family, Judy and Matthew, not hers—I've always looked after them. Only Bambi is hers. Why should she have everything? She'll only make a mess of things.

She remained silent and Sophia said anxiously, "You give it to me, yes, Elinor? What is the trouble? You didn't lose it?"

Would she have told the truth if Sophia hadn't put the idea into her head? Elinor could never decide later.

"I—I didn't know it was important," she mumbled. "I couldn't hear what he said. He hadn't written anything on it. I looked."

"But he say it was a receipt. I am sure that is what he say. What did you do with it? Ellie, you didn't throw it away!" She sprang to her feet. "Where? In the garbage? We look—"

"It got burned."

"Burned? No, no, no! Elinor, you didn't. Tell me it's not true!"

"I thought it was a message," Elinor said, inventing rapidly. "I thought he'd written a secret message on the back of an old ticket, you know, in invisible ink. So when the policewoman told me to make tea, I held the paper over the gas ring to see if the writing would come up and —well, I guess I held it too close."

"You cook it! Your papa give you important receipt and you cook it!" Sophia cried, and added something furiously in Italian, looking as if she wanted to shake Elinor until her head flew off like a football. But then she said contritely, "No. I do not mean it. It's not your fault, Ellie. But how am I going to tell your papa? Perhaps it was not so important . . . You did not notice what the receipt was for, Ellie?"

"No," Elinor said.

Sophia had turned back to her sleeping baby. How pretty she was, Elinor thought. No wonder Dad fell in love with her. No wonder he showered her with presents until all the money was gone; silk and cashmere and diamonds. She saw Sophia's fingers as they tucked the blankets around Bambi. Except for her wedding ring they were bare.

"Where are your diamond rings? Did the police take them?"

"I hide them," Sophia said, looking down at her hands. "They are mine. I am not a criminal. Why should I be punished? Your papa give them to me. They are all I have left now, them and Bambi."

"And us!" Elinor said sharply.

"Yes, of course. You too," Sophia cried, hugging her. "You and Matthew and Judy."

But she forgot us at first, Elinor thought. Perhaps she'd have remembered us later, but I'm glad I lied about the luggage receipt. She's got her diamonds. Why should she have everything?

Chapter Four

MATTHEW DIDN'T trust Sophia. He hadn't been furious, like Ellie, when she first came. Ellie had looked like a sick cat and though he was fond of his sister, he'd felt pleased. Ever since their mother had died, Ellie had bossed him and Judy about, putting on airs like a grown-up. Now her nose was out of joint and a good thing too.

He didn't know why he'd taken against Sophia. Perhaps it was the bird mask she had given him.

"They wear them at carnivals," she'd said. "Everybody wears mask and dresses up and has fun."

He hadn't liked the mask. It was like no bird he had ever seen. A cruel gaping beak. Eyes big as doorknobs. A face glistening red and purple beneath a shiny black crest.

"Put it on! Put it on, Matthew," she'd said.

He'd lifted the mask and set it over his head. Then he stood on a chair so that he could see himself in the mirror over the high mantelpiece. The creature stared back at him, strong, evil, and ugly; growing out of his own thin neck, taking over his own head. And Sophia had laughed and clapped her hands.

"No!" he'd cried, snatching off the mask and throwing it on the floor.

His father had been angry and told him to apologize, but Sophia had said it didn't matter, it was her fault for choosing wrong. She was too nice about it. He didn't trust her. She had charmed his father and Judy, and even won over Ellie. If he hadn't been too old to believe in witches, he'd have thought she'd put a spell on them. But not him. She wasn't going to get him.

Now, after nearly two years, he couldn't think why he had been frightened of the mask. It was great. All his friends admired it. He'd hung it on the wall above his bed to ward off ill luck. But somehow he still didn't trust Sophia. He thought she told lies.

"I'm sorry," she was saying. "You can't come, Matthew. Children are not permitted."

"Are you sure?" he asked, not believing her.

They were in the kitchen, having breakfast. Crumbs littered the table. Last night's dishes were still piled in the sink. Sophia, in her white dressing gown, her feet bare, her chestnut hair uncombed, looked as wild as a gypsy. She was trying to spoon apple puree into Bambi, but the baby kept jerking his head away. Apple puree glistened on his fat cheeks and drooled down his bib. Sophia didn't answer Matthew, but went on making encouraging noises, *"Fai il bravo bambino e mangia la pappa."*

"Are you sure?" Matthew repeated angrily. "Ellie, aren't you going?"

"What?" Elinor asked vaguely. She had been silent all through breakfast, frowning gloomily at her cereal bowl as if suspecting it was poisoned.

"Your papa said not to bring you," Sophia told him. "He doesn't want anyone there—"

"You're going!"

"I'm his wife."

"And I'm his son. I've a right to go."

"I want to go! I want to see Dad!" Judy cried, and Bambi, excited by the noise, waved his arms about and spat apple puree all over his mother.

"Why can't you be good children?" Sophia shouted, close to tears. "It's not suitable for you to come. There is no point. It will be over in five minutes. They commit him for trial and we ask for bail so that he can come home—"

"Come home? When? Today?"

"Perhaps today, perhaps tomorrow," Sophia said. "As soon as things can be arranged."

Ellie looked up at that, opening her mouth as if to ask a question, but then apparently thought better of it. Matthew watched her curiously.

"What were you going to say?" he asked.

"Nothing."

All right, don't tell me, he thought angrily, I won't tell you what I'm going to do. I hope you worry yourself sick, wondering where I've gone.

Sophia, washed and powdered, dressed in a neat black suit, her fiery hair doused beneath a pale silk scarf, went off in a taxi to the court. To Matthew's surprise, neither she nor Ellie had made any fuss when he'd refused to go to Mrs. Crabbe's with Judy and Bambi.

"All right, you can stay here with Elinor, if you like," Sophia had said, and Ellie had shrugged and said nothing.

As soon as the door had shut behind Sophia, he put on his parka. Ellie watched him. She still said nothing but merely smiled and opened the front door again.

"Aren't you going to ask where I'm going?" he said, made uneasy by her unusual behavior.

"You're going to the magistrates' court," she said, as if she could see right into his head. "I don't think they'll let you in, but you can try. You'd better hurry in case Dad's on first. Good luck."

He felt oddly deflated. He wished she'd forbidden him to go, so that he could have rushed off in a temper, without time to think. The magistrates' court was in Church Street, a good fifteen minutes' walk. . . . He hated going into rooms late, with everyone turning around to stare.

"Come with me," he said.

"I can't. I'm going out."

"Where?"

She smiled. "I didn't ask you that. Don't be nosy, Matt. Good-bye."

He went out and she shut the door behind him. The taxi was out of sight. He ran down to the corner and then looked back in time to see his sister come out of the house. She was wearing a navy jacket over her denim trousers, and had a long white scarf around her neck. She stood on the pavement outside their gate and looked carefully up and down the street. When she saw him, she waved and pointed to her wrist to remind him of the time. He waved back and went around the corner.

What was she up to? He walked on slowly down Main Street, then ducked into the baker's shop. It was crowded and he stood at the end of the line, looking sideways out of the window. Of course, she might go the other way, down the hill—no, here she was, walking briskly now, her eyes bright and nervous. Where could she be going? He decided to find out.

"Excuse me, are you in the line?" a woman asked. He shook his head, mumbled something, and left the shop.

Ellie wasn't easy to follow. She kept looking around, forcing him to dodge behind people or into shop door-ways. He let the gap between them widen and saw her cross the road and turn into Southwood Lane.

There were no shops here. No people. Nowhere to hide, if she looked around. He hesitated, biting his thumb. Then two bulky women passed him and turned into Southwood Lane and he followed gratefully in their shadow. Between their chattering heads he saw Ellie half-way down the road, her white scarf blowing in the wind like a pennant. She still kept glancing over her shoulder. He thought she looked nervous.

He was afraid the two women might stop at one of the houses on the way, but they walked down the hill as if fate had arranged for them to be his shield. When Ellie reached the bottom, she was hidden by people coming up the hill. He began to run, frightened he'd lost her. Then he saw her, on the other side of the main road, her white scarf still blowing in the wind. As he watched, she turned and ran down the steps to the subway station.

The lights were against him. Everything was against him. When he finally got across the road, an old lady blocked his way, a dog ran between his legs and nearly tripped him up, he had no money to buy a ticket. He ran past the man at the barrier, saying wildly, "My sister! Got to tell her something!" and went bounding down the es-calator. The man looked after him and shrugged.

Where was Ellie going? Left to Mill Hill and Edgware? Right to the West End or the City? He turned right—and there she was on the platform, looking straight at him and smiling.

"I got you a ticket, Matt," she said. "I know you never have any money."

He stared at her and she burst out laughing.

"Did you guess I'd follow you?" he asked, when they were sitting side by side on the train.

"No."

"But you kept looking around."

"Oh, I had a feeling," she said vaguely. "And then in Southwood Lane, I saw two women with three heads. And one of them was yours."

He smiled. "Where are we going?"

"I know where I'm going. I don't know if you're coming with me. I didn't mean you to."

"Why? What are you doing? It's something to do with Dad, isn't it? Let me come. I won't tell," he promised. "You know I won't. I've never told on you, have I? Please, Ellie."

He had no idea what she was up to, but he wanted to be part of it. All last night he'd had bad dreams, running from one dark nightmare to another, shouting for help and nobody answering. He was glad to be sitting in the warm, rattling train next to his sister, going he didn't know where. Ellie was bossy but he trusted her.

"If you let me come," he said, "I won't even ask any questions, if you don't want me to."

"Won't you?" She looked at him thoughtfully and then

made up her mind. "All right. I can do with company. Only, if you ever tell anyone, I'll cut your throat."

"I won't," Matt promised.

"Nobody. Not Sophia, not Judy," she said, and added, to his surprise, "not even Dad. Somebody's got to look after the three of us."

Chapter Five

THEY CAME out of the subway into Victoria Station, along with about a hundred other people, adding fresh confusion to the crowds already there. Ellie walked quickly so that Matthew had to hurry to keep up with her. It would be easy to get lost. People kept pushing between them, people carrying suitcases, knapsacks, babies; checking their tickets, counting their children.

It was a place for journeys, beginning and ending, a traveler's place. Were they going to run away? I wouldn't mind, he thought, for trains excited him. But Ellie would never leave Judy behind.

"Where are we going?" he asked.

"To the baggage-claim office," she told him. "I've got to collect something."

"What?"

"I don't know," she said with a nervous giggle. "Could be anything; a parcel, an umbrella, a stuffed parrot . . . Whatever it is, we mustn't look surprised. I don't suppose they'll remember who left it there. I hope not. I wish I looked older."

"Don't you have to have a receipt or something?" he asked.

"I've got one." She pulled it out of her pocket and showed it to him. He looked at it curiously. "It's a bit creased. Where did you get it?"

"Hey, no questions!" she said quickly. "You promised. Look, there it is, over there."

She pulled him out of the hurrying crowd into a quiet space by a pillar, from which they could see the baggage-claim office. There was only one man behind the counter, a middle-aged man who looked as if his breakfast had disagreed with him and his feet hurt.

"I wish there were some other customers," Elinor muttered. Matthew could tell she was nervous. Her eyes were bright but restless. She kept looking around as if afraid of what she might see.

"Do you think we are being followed?" he asked.

"No. Not really. I'm just being silly."

"There're two policemen over there."

"I know. I saw them. There are always policemen at big railway stations. They're not even looking this way. Come on."

The man behind the counter scarcely looked at them. They weren't people to him, just work, Matthew thought. A hand holding out a piece of paper, a suitcase thumped down on the counter, over and over again, day after day.

"We've still got to be careful," Elinor said, as they hurried away. "I won't feel safe until . . ." Her voice trailed away as if, looking forward, she couldn't see a time when she would ever feel safe again. Her smile faded.

Matthew felt cold. His eyes went to the case she was

carrying. It was a small overnight case, ordinary, dark gray, and plain. There were no initials on it but he didn't need any to guess whose it was.

"I was wrong about Dad, wasn't I?" he said bitterly. "He is a thief, a stinking thief!"

"Shut up!" she muttered fiercely. "For God's sake, calm down. You promised—"

"Oh, I won't tell," he said. "Do you think I want everyone to know?"

They would be bound to know sooner or later. It would be in the papers. His friends at school would sympathize and his enemies would gloat, and he didn't know which would be hardest to bear. Every time anything was missing, they would look at him.

I hate him, he thought, always pretending to be so perfect. *He* never did anything wrong, oh no! It was always me. The fuss he made that day when he found me shaking a few coins out of Ellie's piggy bank and I was only five then. Poor Ellie, she always thought he was so wonderful. I wonder what she thinks now. Not that she'll let on. . . .

"How much did he steal?" he asked.

"Shut up!"

They went home by subway. Ellie sat with the case on her lap and her arms resting on the top. No wonder she looked worried. There must be thousands in there. Millions, perhaps. The thought fascinated him. He couldn't take his eyes off the case.

"What are you going to do with it?" he whispered.

"Hide it."

"Where?"

She looked at him sideways but didn't answer. Didn't

she trust him? She had to. They were in it together. He looked at the people opposite and thought one or two of them glanced quickly away. Three youths were whispering together. A woman in a blue coat stared straight at Ellie. A man caught his eye and ducked behind his newspaper.

As the train slowed down for Kentish Town, Matthew whispered urgently, "Let's get out of here."

"Why?"

"Everybody's looking at us."

"No, they're not. Calm down. Do you want to play ticktacktoe or something?"

"No," he said angrily, turning away.

After a minute he felt her hand on his arm. "Matt, I need your help," she whispered.

He didn't answer, recognizing this for what it was. Soft soap. Flatter your little brother. Appeal to his better instincts.

"Do you know you need money to get bail?" she whispered. He could not help his head turning and his eyes going back to the case on her lap.

"Is that why you fetched it today?"

"Yes."

"But who will you give it to? The court? Supposing they ask you where you got it from?"

"That's just it. I can't very well claim I got it out of my piggy bank, can I? I've been stupid. I might just as well have left it where it was. What shall I do, Matt?"

He smiled, won over by her treating him as an equal. He'd always resented the four years between them, hated being lumped together with Judy, just because they were closer in age. "Your little brother and sister," Sophia often said, when talking to Ellie.

"Does Sophia know about it?" he asked.

"No."

"Don't tell her!"

"I won't. Not yet. Only if we have to."

"We'll think of something," he said and, leaning close to her, whispered in her ear, "I know of a good hiding place for it."

They came home through the back garden and hid the case between the garden shed and the wall, not knowing who might be in the house to see them come out of the shrubs and cross the lawn. The kitchen door was locked. They walked along the terrace and peered in through the French windows. At the far end of the room Sophia was sitting at the table, her head in her hands. Beside her was a short plump man, with a pink face and smooth dark hair. Elinor tapped on the glass.

They both looked around and then got to their feet. Sophia came and let them in.

"Good," she said. "You have come back. Here is Mr. Brimly, who you know, yes?" She smiled at them, but they saw that she had been crying.

"What happened?" Elinor asked.

The lawyer glanced at Sophia and then said, "Much as we expected. We agreed to the short committal. Your father will come up for trial in a month or so, and then it will be over. The waiting is usually the worst part," he said, looking at them kindly.

"When's Dad coming home?" Matthew asked.

"I'm afraid we struck a small hitch there," Mr. Brimly

said, putting some papers back in his briefcase. "The magistrates have refused to grant bail. The police advised against it. It didn't exactly help that both your father's partners are no longer in the country."

"But we can pay for bail," Elinor cried. "I mean, we can get the money—"

"It's not a question of money," he told her. "But don't worry too much. We're going to appeal against their decision. Until then we'll have to be patient."

The case was locked. They smuggled it into the house later that night, when Judy and Bambi were in bed, and Sophia on the telephone, and hid it under the loose floorboards in Matthew's room.

"How much do you think is in there?" Matthew whispered.

"I don't know," Elinor said, rolling the carpet back carefully, pressing the edges into the crack beneath the skirting so that nobody would notice it had been disturbed. "It might not be money. It might be papers."

"Or diamonds," Matthew suggested. "Or gold."

"Not heavy enough. Get into bed, Matt, and I'll tuck you in. You look exhausted."

He was pale and his eyes were overbright. She wished she hadn't taken him to Victoria, hadn't told him about the suitcase. He'd tried to pick the locks with the point of his compass, and then a pair of scissors, but neither of them knew how to do it. He would have forced the lock if she hadn't stopped him.

"We mustn't damage it. It isn't ours."

"Dad doesn't worry about things like that," he'd said.

"Why should we?" She hadn't known what to say to that, so pretended not to hear.

Later, back in her own room, she thought about it. It was true. Why should she feel guilty about the lie she'd told Sophia? It was only a little thing. It didn't matter. She could tell him the truth when she visited him. She could whisper it to him when they kissed. Did they let fathers kiss their children in prison?

It never occurred to Elinor that her father would refuse to let her come with Sophia to visit him.

"I don't believe you! You're lying!" she shouted.

"Perhaps next time he say you can come," she said.

"Perhaps next time I won't want to!" Elinor retorted, and refused to be comforted. Let her father think the receipt was burned. It wasn't his money, anyway. Serve him right if she spent it all. But when Sophia came back, she could not help asking about it.

"Did you tell him about the receipt?"

"Yes. It was difficult because there is a warder in the room, but I pretend to cry and I say it in Italian with my eyes up to the ceiling like I am praying."

"What did Dad say?"

"Nothing. He just sit there like someone punch all the wind out of him. He does not look like my Georgio anymore. He look like an old man."

Chapter Six

THE WEATHER turned colder. On April first, like a bad joke, there was a fall of hailstones, rattling against the windows and knocking over the daffodils. Then in the night it snowed, a wet, sloppy snow, already dripping down from the trees when they woke, and graying to slush on the pavements. Bambi had a bad cold.

"I hate this country," Sophia muttered.

"It'll be better soon," Elinor told her. "It'll be lovely next week, you'll see."

"Next week may be too late."

"Bambi's only got a cold. He won't die of it. He's getting better already. Wait till the sun comes out—"

"If it ever does," Sophia said gloomily.

"Wait and see," Elinor said, forcing herself to sound cheerful.

Wait. It was all they had to do now. Wait to see if the appeals judge would allow Dad bail after all so that he could come home. Wait for the trial. Wait for the Housing Authority to find them somewhere to live before they were turned out of the house. Wait.

It got on everyone's nerves. Sophia was irritable and

Bambi cried all day. Judy quarreled with Matthew and Matthew was rude to Sophia. Elinor told her friend Annabel she'd go mad trying to keep the peace.

"Why do you bother?" Annabel asked. "Let them fight. If Sophia doesn't like it, let her stop them. She's their stepmother, not you."

"Dad asked me to look after them," Elinor said.

"You don't have to do what your father tells you now," Annabel said. "He's hardly in a position to tell you off, is he?"

"No," Elinor agreed.

She didn't confess to Annabel that what she wanted most of all was someone to tell her what to do. Annabel didn't have a father in prison awaiting trial. Annabel didn't have a young stepmother who complained every day about the weather in England, and phoned her mother in Naples every night, talking for ages in a language Elinor couldn't understand but out of which her own name occasionally floated "Elinor."

"What were you saying about me?" she would ask, but Sophia always said she could not remember.

Sophia was up to something, Elinor was certain of it. This was her real reason for not wanting Matthew and Judy to upset her. It was something to do with them. Something that made Sophia look at her stepchildren with a mixture of irritation and remorse, as if she knew they wouldn't like what she was about to do and was getting ready to shout down their objections. Once, coming in to say good-night, she'd hugged Elinor and said, her voice muffled in Elinor's long hair, "I love you and Matthew and Judy. I try to do what is best for you."

But when Elinor asked hopefully, "Then can I come

with you when you visit Dad?" her mood changed abruptly.

"Oh, you're so difficult," she cried. "Why do you keep asking? I tell you again and again. Your papa say no. He does not want his children to see him in prison."

"He should have thought of that before," Elinor said angrily, but Sophia had already slammed out of the room.

"Do you believe that about Dad?" Matthew asked, when she told him what Sophia had said. "She tells lies, you know. Still, I suppose it could be true. If I was in trouble at school, I certainly wouldn't want you characters coming along. I'd rather get it over on my own. Dad always hates being in the wrong, even in little things."

"He may not be in the wrong. He hasn't been found guilty yet."

"Come off it, Ellie. What d'you think is in the case, Dad's pajamas?"

"Could be."

"I bet. Let's open it and see," he tempted. "I could force the lock easily." It wasn't the first time he'd suggested it. At first Elinor had been tempted, but not now. She had begun to hate the case. She felt it was like a Pandora's box that, once opened, would let out a swarm of horrors into their world.

"I'd better hide it somewhere else, if I can't trust you to keep your hands off it," she said.

"Oh, I won't touch the beastly thing," he told her sulkily. "Though what you're waiting for, I don't know. Dad can't write and tell you what to do with it in case they open his letters, and we can't get in to see him."

They had tried. Since Sophia wouldn't take them, they

had gone to the prison themselves, only to be turned away. Children were only allowed to visit when accompanied by an adult, they were told, kindly enough. They had stood on the opposite side of the road, from where the top of the prison showed above the high walls, outlined against the sky. Elinor, looking down at Matthew's pale face, had said cheerfully, "Looks just like the apartment building where our piano teacher used to live, doesn't it? Come on, let's buy some chocolate to eat on the bus going home."

"Perhaps we can get someone to take us in," she said now. "Not Sophia. Someone like—" She broke off as the door opened and Judy came into the room. "Hello, I thought you were next door. I didn't hear you come in."

"I came over the garden wall," Judy said, sounding pleased with herself. "Sophia let me in through the kitchen. What are you two talking about?"

"Nothing," they said quickly, for Judy was like an echo and repeated everything she was told.

"What's that you're eating?" Elinor asked to distract her, for she was looking suspicious.

"A cookie. Sophia's making them. She only let me have one, the piggy woman. She says they're for tomorrow."

"What's happening tomorrow?"

Judy shrugged. "It isn't a party. I asked. She says it's just some people coming and I don't have to be there till lunch. I can go next door if they ask me again."

Matthew and Elinor looked at each other, puzzled and uneasy. Matthew opened his mouth to ask a question but Elinor frowned at him, a frown plainly meaning, not now. Not in front of Judy.

Judy noticed. You could never tell with her. She seemed young for her age, dreamy, almost a little simple. At seven, she still put on the pretty-baby act that had done so well for her when she was small. But sometimes, like now, Elinor noticed a shrewd look in her sister's big blue eyes, the look of a girl who knew which side of her bread was buttered—and where the honey was hidden.

"I won't go next door tomorrow, even if they ask me," she said, looking at them out of the corner of her eyes, "I think I'll go to Sophia's party. I bet it is a party, don't you?" Her face brightened suddenly. "Perhaps Daddy's coming home."

"No, of course he is not coming home tomorrow," Sophia said. "What gave her that idea? Because I make cookies? Your papa doesn't even like my cookies. He say they are like spiced sawdust."

It was late. Matthew and Judy were asleep in their rooms. Bambi snuffled and snored in his cot. Elinor had sat up, waiting for Sophia to come back from next door. She had switched on all the lights but their artificial glitter could not comfort her. She was glad when Sophia came in, shaking the thin snow out of her wet hair.

"I'm sorry I'm late," she said, throwing her coat down on one chair and herself on another. "They want to know everything and how can I say no? They are so kind looking after Bambi and Judy. I have to tell them."

"I'm kind looking after Bambi and Judy, but you don't tell me much," Elinor said. "You used to tell me, we used to talk a lot. You said it was like having a younger sister. But you've changed."

"Everything's changed," Sophia said with a shiver,

though the room was warm. "And you are only thirteen even though I sometimes forget this. It isn't right to let you worry."

"It's worse not knowing," Elinor burst out. "Nothing could be as bad as the things I imagine. Why doesn't Dad want us to visit him? Is he ill? Is he—"

"He is well, I promise you," Sophia said quickly, coming and sitting beside Elinor on the sofa. "Always he sends his love and says we are not to worry. Only—everything is so difficult. He says now he does not want bail, after all. He has told Mr. Brimly not to appeal. He will stay in prison until the trial."

"Why?" Elinor asked, feeling horribly guilty. "Is it because of money? Because I have—"

"No, no!" Sophia interrupted her before she could confess. "I asked. I offered to sell my diamonds but Mr. Brimly says it isn't that. It is hard for your papa. He was so successful, so—so important in his business. He was the youngest director, that was something to be proud of. I think he is ashamed to show his face to the neighbors." She looked angry for a moment and said bitterly, "But what about our faces? We have the reporters and people staring and asking questions like next door. Mr. Brimly says prison is hard for a man like Georgio, but it is hard for us too. Mr. Brimly says we cannot stay here, we must find somewhere. I go to the Housing Authority, but they have no houses for us. They say when we are turned out into the street, they will put us in bed and breakfast place —I have seen them on TV. They are damp and horrible and not healthy for babies. It's not what I want for Bambi."

"We'll find somewhere to go," Elinor said. "We'll be all right. I'll help you, Sophia. I've got the money—"

It was the second time she nearly told Sophia about the suitcase but again Sophia interrupted her. It wasn't money, she told Elinor. She was used to being poor. They had been poor at home in Napoli, but it was different there. They had been all poor together and the sun shone.

"It was warm," she said.

No good telling her April could be warm in England, too, that it could be a lovely month. They sat in silence, listening to the sleet blowing against the windows.

"You were right, Ellie," Sophia said at last. "What you say when I first come, remember? You say I am too young to be a stepmother. It's true. I'm sorry but I can't— Bambi isn't well. He coughs all the time, and I want to take him home to my mama. He is her grandchild. She has never seen him yet."

She talked quickly, her words tumbling over one another, looking at Elinor with that half-defiant, half-remorseful look. Elinor said nothing. "You know I love you," Sophia went on. "But how can I take you with me, big children like you? We have only a little apartment, already crowded. But you will be all right. I have arranged for you to be looked after while I am gone."

"Is that who the cookies are for?" Elinor asked. "The people from Child Welfare?"

Sophia looked at her blankly. "It is nothing to do with Child Welfare. I telephoned your relatives and they are coming tomorrow."

"Our relatives?" Elinor repeated in amazement. "But

we never see them. Dad said they were a terrible, dreary lot."

"That is not what he say to me. He say they are good people. He say blood is thicker than water—"

"He said that to me once," Elinor interrupted. "He said blood is thicker than water and a lot harder to stomach."

"I don't understand," Sophia said stiffly. "They are your family. Of course they help."

"I thought you and Bambi were our family once," Elinor said, and remained stony faced, even when Sophia cried, and said it was only for a short time, until Bambi was better, until she could find them somewhere to live —she would come back soon.

"Please don't trouble on our account," Elinor said coldly. "We can manage on our own."

Chapter Seven

THEY SAT by the window in Judy's room, watching the road, waiting for their relatives to come. Downstairs Sophia was vacuuming the hall, buzzing about like an angry wasp. She had asked them to help her tidy up, and they had refused, saying, "You asked them, not us."

"Perhaps I'd better go and help her," Elinor said. "They'll be here any minute."

"No, don't, Ellie!" Matthew cried, and Judy echoed him, catching hold of her hand, "Don't go, Ellie. Stay with us."

They were both uneasy. Matthew could not remember their relatives clearly. Judy said she could not remember them at all.

"They never came to see me," she complained.

"They did when you were a baby. And one of Dad's cousins came to stay with us later. Agnes. Agnes something—don't you remember?"

"No. What was she like?"

A small woman, Elinor remembered, with a weather-beaten face and short dark hair, homemade clothes and clumpy shoes. She'd come up when their mother was ill and offered to look after them all. Dad had soon got rid of her. Mom had trained nurses looking after her and Agnes had only got under their feet, running upstairs with peppermint tea and sorrel soup and pungent herbal remedies.

"She was kind," Elinor said, not wanting to put Judy off. "She used to send us presents at Christmas. I don't know why she stopped. Perhaps because we never wrote and thanked her."

"Or because she's dead," Matthew suggested.

"Then this must be her ghost."

A taxi had stopped outside their house. Agnes whatever-her-name-was got out of the back. She hadn't changed much, except that her face was less red than Elinor remembered and her clothes less peculiar, a plain blue parka and black trousers. They watched her pay off the taxi and walk quickly up the path to the front door. She did not look up.

"Shall I throw my pillow on her head?" Judy asked, leaning out of the window. "She looks horrible. I'm not going to stay with *her.* I hate her."

"She hasn't offered to have us yet," Elinor said, pulling her sister back. "And if she heard you, she won't. Anyway, it's only for a short time, until Sophia comes back."

"If she ever does," Matthew said.

Judy began to cry and Elinor shouted at them both. By the time they'd all calmed down again, they'd missed the arrival of Aunt Cathy, their father's sister, and were only just in time to see a sad, meek-looking man, with half his hair worn away on top, holding a green umbrella over someone beside him.

"I don't like them either," Judy said. "Who are they?"

"I think they must be Dad's cousins from Worthing," Elinor told her. "Bob and Louise Shaw. I went to stay with them once, ages ago. They never asked me again."

They had spent the days on the beach, and Elinor had caught the sun painfully across her shoulders, turning bright red. There'd been two boys about her own age who'd kept slapping her on the back, and shrieking with laughter when she winced. Elinor had put up with it for a time and then told Mrs. Shaw. It hadn't done her any good. Mrs. Shaw told her she didn't like children who told tales.

"I didn't think they'd come," she said, frowning. "Is that the lot, do you think? We'd better go down."

Judy threw her doll on the floor and ran over to the mirror, fluffing out her hair and turning this way and that. Matthew was reluctant.

"Sophia said she'd call us," he said. "She said we were to wait until she called us."

"I expect they want to talk about us behind our backs." Elinor smiled. "Let's go down and spoil their fun."

The living-room door was open a little. As they crossed the hall, their feet silent on the thick carpet, they heard a woman's voice say, "If you ask me, it really is the limit. We haven't heard from George for years. The moment he became successful, he couldn't drop us fast enough. He just didn't want to know. We weren't good enough for his new friends. Now that he's in trouble, of course, it's a different story. Now the family are expected to rally round. I couldn't believe my ears when you telephoned.

We didn't even know George had married again. He didn't bother to invite us to his wedding. And now he wants our help. Well, I'm afraid I don't see it that way—"

"Why did you come here, then?" Elinor demanded, pushing the door wide open. "If you were just going to be horrible about Dad, you should've stayed at home."

They all turned around, and she stared back at them, prepared, like Judy, to hate them all.

"We don't need you," Elinor said rudely. "We can look after ourselves."

There was a short, astonished silence. Then Aunt Cathy stepped forward. She was their father's only sister, a tall woman with fine gray eyes like his and dark hair, her face heavily made up and her perfume so strong that they could smell it from where they stood. They did not know her very well. She had married a Canadian and gone to live in Toronto, and hadn't invited them to visit her, though she sent them occasional presents and photographs of Niagara Falls. After her divorce she had returned to England and bought an apartment on the other side of London. Elinor had spoken to her on the telephone. "I'm longing to see you all again, my dear," Aunt Cathy had said. "Just give me time to straighten myself out." That had been two months ago, and here she was at last, holding out her arms and saying, "My poor, poor darlings."

They hesitated, uncertain how to respond to this theatrical greeting. Then Elinor walked stiffly forward, to be hugged and kissed and finally held at arm's length to be inspected.

("It was like a cattle auction," she told her friend Annabel later. "I expected at any moment to be prodded and to have my teeth examined.")

"How you've grown," her aunt said. "You must be— what? Fourteen?"

"Thirteen."

"And these two—Matthew, isn't it? And this must be Judy. You were only a baby when I saw you last. What a little beauty you've grown into. Such lovely hair," Aunt Cathy said, running a strand through her fingers like silk.

("As if wondering how much it had cost," Elinor told Annabel later.)

Judy loved being made a fuss of. She sat next to Aunt Cathy at lunch, chattering away, knowing instinctively, Elinor thought with amusement, which of their relatives was the creampot. But was Aunt Cathy prepared to take them all? she wondered.

No.

"If only I didn't have such a tiny little apartment," Aunt Cathy said apologetically. "I'd love to take you all. But I really can't fit in more than a small one." She smiled at Judy, who suddenly looked uncertain, not having thought they might be separated.

"We want to stay together," Elinor said loudly.

"Beggars can't be choosers, I'm afraid." It was Mrs. Shaw who said this, with a splintery little laugh. She was a bottle-blonde, with small eyes and a pointed nose, whom Elinor remembered only too well. "My husband says we can take the boy, if no one else wants him. He can go in with our two. But what about his schooling? The summer term starts next Wednesday."

"They will miss a week or two," Sophia said, shrugging. "When I come back, I do something. I find somewhere."

She had been subdued, uneasy with these in-laws who looked at her with such obvious disapproval. Even Bambi in his high chair was quiet, as if he sensed they didn't approve of him either.

"I'd have thought you could have postponed your visit home until you'd got things like that settled," Aunt Cathy said. "I suppose they went to private schools? That's out of the question now, I imagine."

"There is no money," Sophia said.

As Mrs. Shaw began talking, Matthew whispered in Elinor's ear, "We've got money. Can't we live somewhere by ourselves, Ellie?"

"They wouldn't let us."

"I don't want to go to that woman," he said.

She didn't blame him, but what could she do? "It'd only be for a short time," she whispered. "And *he's* nice."

"What about you? Where will you go?"

"I don't know. Nobody wants me," she said, and smiled to hide the fact that it hurt.

She had thought that she could've stayed with Annabel, had even hoped that Annabel's parents would invite the three of them, because of course she couldn't go without Matthew and Judy. In fact Annabel had suggested it, only to come around the next day with an embarrassed face, saying that her parents were expecting guests and there wouldn't be room. "Don't they want you to see me anymore, now that Dad's in prison?" Elinor had asked bitterly.

"Don't be silly. It isn't that."

"What is it, then?"

"They think it might be difficult if . . ."

"If what?" Elinor had demanded, as Annabel hesitated.

"If your stepmother never comes back."

It had frightened her. Not for herself, she'd be all right. "You're the strong one in the family," her father had said. But Matthew and Judy—she'd always looked after them since their mother died. We must stay together, she thought.

She looked around the table. Judy was leaning against Aunt Cathy, who smiled down at her and whispered something that made Judy laugh. Matthew was talking to Mr. Shaw. He looked animated, his dark eyes shining. They were talking about boats. Mr. Shaw was promising to take Matthew out fishing. . . .

"We've got to stay together," she said stubbornly. "You can't split us up."

They all looked at her.

"But, Ellie, like you said, it's only for a short time. Till Sophia comes back," Matthew said. He seemed to have forgotten his fears.

"Aunt Cathy's going to take me to see a play," Judy said. "I want to go, Ellie. I'm going to sleep in a brass bed."

Elinor flushed and bit her lip.

Then the small woman, who had been silent up till then, leaned forward.

"We have an attic room," Agnes Carter said. "I'm afraid it's very small and cramped, and gets terribly hot in summer. . . . But you're very welcome, Elinor, if you'd like to come and stay with us. You'd be company for Timon."

Chapter Eight

THERE WAS nothing Elinor could do about it. They were to be handed around like Sophia's cookies; Judy to Aunt Cathy in Fulham, Matthew to the Shaws in Worthing, and Elinor to the Carters in a dim-sounding place called Nettlewood in Wiltshire.

Judy had already gone, clutching a new doll and looking back over her shoulder as Aunt Cathy led her away. She had cried at the last moment, clinging to Elinor and whispering that she didn't want to go.

"Ssh! She'll hear you. You'll be all right," Elinor comforted her. "You'll have a lovely time."

She wasn't worried about Judy. Judy always landed on her feet, like a clever little kitten. She seemed to know by instinct how to endear herself to grown-ups. It was Matthew Elinor worried about.

"Tell him he must pack today," Sophia said.

They were having breakfast in the kitchen again. They never used the dining room now. Sophia's eyes were heavy with sleeplessness and old tears. She had been up in the night, Elinor had heard Bambi crying and footsteps passing her door, but she hadn't got up to help as she once would have done. She used to make Sophia hot chocolate in the middle of the night, bad for the teeth but warm for the heart. They had taken it in turns to carry Bambi up and down the room until he'd fallen asleep again. . . .

"Tell Matthew it is not good to behave like this," Sophia was saying. "If he refuses to pack, I must do it for him and I will put in the wrong things. I don't know what people wear in Worthing."

"Does she think Worthing's on the moon?" Matthew asked Elinor loudly. "Tell her I'll pack for myself. When I feel like it."

"Tell her yourself," Elinor said.

She was tired of the game he was playing. Ever since Judy had left, he'd refused to speak to Sophia directly. At first Sophia had shrugged and left him alone. Then it had gotten on her nerves and she'd tried coaxing, shouting, once she'd even hit him, a stinging slap across the cheek, only to burst into tears when he'd turned to Elinor and said coldly, "Tell her I'll never forgive her for that."

Since then they had been stiffly polite, talking to one another through Elinor—"Tell her I can't find any clean pajamas." "Ask him if he's looked in the linen closet—I always put them there." It might have been funny, but it wasn't.

"I wish you'd stop doing it," Elinor told Matthew. She'd come up to his room as soon as Sophia had gone out, and offered to help him pack. It ended up with her doing it all, while he watched her moodily. "It's cruel," she said. "It's like pulling wings off flies. I can't help feeling sorry for her. I think she's coming to pieces. She cries every night, both she and Bambi. They wake me up."

He shrugged. "Bambi's teething."

"I know, but she isn't. She's just unhappy. And it's not her fault, any of it."

"Dad wasn't a criminal till she came."

She sat back on her heels and stared at him. So that's what he thought. Poor Sophia.

"I think it started before he met her," she said slowly. "Probably before we moved here—this is a far posher house than the one we had in Finchley, and he made us change schools. That's when he started throwing money around—" She broke off and looked at the corner of the room, where the carpet covered the loose floorboards. "Talking about money, we can't leave that there. The house isn't ours. They're only letting us stay here because we've got nowhere to go. As soon as she's got us off her hands, she's going to sell half the furniture and store the rest."

"And she pretends she's coming back! There'll be nowhere to come back to. This won't be my room anymore." Matthew looked around and caught sight of the bird mask above his bed. "She's put a jinx on us!" he cried angrily. "She's brought us nothing but bad luck."

He jumped up on the bed and pulled the mask down from the wall.

"What are you going to do with it?" Elinor asked, for his face looked as fierce as the bird's.

"Destroy it! Burn it! I know, let's make a funeral pyre in the garden."

The mask was an expensive one. It would be like burning money. Money, Elinor thought, and she saw flames, clean and bright, destroying the stolen money, burning away her father's guilt. Everything going up in smoke and the smoke drifting away, leaving the sky clear.

"Let's burn the money too," she said.

"Ellie!"

She'd thought it was the sort of wild idea that might appeal to him. He was always complaining that she was too sensible. Dull. Boring. Those were the words he threw at her when they quarreled. But now he stared at her as if she was out of her mind.

"You can't mean it," he said.

She sighed. "No, not really. It's just—I'm beginning to hate it. I don't know what to do with it. It doesn't belong to us. Nor to Dad."

"It must belong to someone."

"I suppose so. I don't know. I don't really care."

They meant nothing to her, the hundreds of people who had invested in her father's company and lost every penny. They weren't real to her. They had no faces.

"We'd better move it now while Sophia's out," she said. "We might not get another chance. I'll put it with my luggage. Come on."

They rolled back the carpet, and Matthew levered up the loose floorboards with his penknife. The suitcase was still there, covered with a thin sprinkling of dust. Matthew brought it out and laid it on the floor between them.

"I can force the locks easily. It wouldn't even show."

She pulled the case away before he could touch it. "No. It would turn us into a kind of thief. Accessories. Receivers of stolen goods. As long as the case is locked, we are innocent, see? Nobody can blame us. How are we to know what's inside? We wouldn't dream of forcing the lock, would we? That would be damaging other people's property and they're always telling us not to do that."

He couldn't tell from her voice whether she was serious or not.

"What are you going to do with it, then?"

"I'll take it with me to Nettlewood until I know what Dad wants me to do with it."

"What Dad wants! Why not what we want for a change? He didn't worry about us, did he? Judy told me. She said he was already dressed and packed up ready to go, when the police came and stopped him. He was going to leave us behind, Ellie."

"He'd have sent for us later."

"How do you know? Did he tell you that?" Matthew demanded. She didn't answer, so he went on. "He cheated those people, so how do you know he wouldn't have cheated us too? Why do you keep sticking up for him?"

"I don't know," she confessed. "Only—we're all he's got left, Matt, now that Sophia's leaving. Somebody's got to go on loving him. Okay, perhaps he is a rat, but we're not perfect either, and he's always forgiven us. Remember when you were in trouble at school? And when I lost the important letter he'd given me to mail? And Judy—"

"Oh, Judy has only to cry and he'd forgive her murder," Matthew said. "All right, I get your point. Family loyalty and all that. It still makes me sick, though. And why won't he let us visit him?"

"I don't know."

They were silent for a moment, then Elinor said, "I wrote to him again, you know."

They had written to him before, careful letters, giving nothing away.

"We know you didn't do anything wrong, Dad," they wrote untruthfully, and "Let us know if there's anything you want us to do for you." He had not written back, but merely sent his love.

"Any luck this time?" Matthew asked.

"No. Just the same as before. Another message through Sophia. He's well and he sends his love. Oh, there was something new."

"What?"

"He asked her to tell us he was sorry."

"Sorry!" Matthew cried. He threw the bird mask on the floor and jumped on it, stamping his feet up and down until it was reduced to tiny fragments of *papier-mâché,* the doorknob eyes, the fierce beak, the purple face all gone, as harmless now as crumbs on the carpet.

Chapter Nine

ELINOR FELT lonely after Matthew had gone. She was not due to go to Nettlewood until Saturday. Annabel was away, and she did not feel like facing her other friends and their questions. Every morning she begged Sophia to let her come to the prison, but the answer was always the same. No. It was not possible. Her papa did not wish it.

"Why not? Is he cross with me because I burned the receipt?"

"No, of course not."

"Why, then?"

"He say you will understand."

"I don't," Elinor said flatly, and Sophia sighed and confessed that she didn't either. It was very odd.

"Mr. Brimly say we must be patient. He say prison takes some people like that. They want to hide, they don't want to see anyone. You do not miss much, Ellie. The visits they are not so very nice. Fifteen minutes a day, that is all. I think at first I will not be able to say all I want in this short time, but I am wrong. It takes me about ten minutes, perhaps, and then we sit and I see him look at the clock, and I want to cry."

"Doesn't he talk about us at all?"

"Yes, yes, of course. Always he ask after you and send his love and I give him all your messages. But I think the prison clock is slow."

"If you take me, I can talk for ages—" Elinor said, but it was no good.

So on Friday, after Sophia had gone out with Bambi, she went to the prison by herself. She sat in the bus, looking hopefully at the other passengers, wondering how many were going her way, and whether any would be willing to smuggle her in with them. But when the bus stopped, she was the only person to get off. Perhaps she was too early, or too late.

From this side of the road it was possible to see the top of the prison above the high walls. Painted a pale sandy color, it looked warm and cheerful in the thin April sunlight. Only the tall blackened chimney struck an odd, sinister note, though it was probably only the prison laundry.

She gazed up at the high barred windows but could see no pale prisoners looking down. People passing her on the pavement glanced at her curiously and then up at the prison and walked on. Only one person stopped, a slow old lady with a pink knitted hat and a bag full of shopping.

"That's the prison," she said.

"I know."

"Got someone inside or just curious?"

"My father's in there," Elinor said.

"Oh, that's a shame, dear." The old lady took out a handkerchief and blew her nose on a sympathetic note.

"Never mind. The time soon passes. This your first visit, dear? The entrance is over there." She pointed.

"They won't let me in," Elinor told her. "They say I've got to have an adult accompanying me."

"Like at the movies," the old lady said, nodding her head. "I remember. They wouldn't let us in to some films without we had an adult with us. We'd hang about outside the Odeon and ask anyone with a kind face to take us in—" She broke off and began to back away. "Oh no, dear, it ain't no good you looking at me all hopeful. I can't take you in. We wouldn't get away with it and then where would we be? In the clink, that's where." She gave a little squeal of laughter at her joke and repeated it in case Elinor had missed it, "In the clink, see?"

"You could say you were my grandma."

"No, I couldn't, dear. It wouldn't be honest," the old lady said nervously, and hurried away on her painful old feet.

Elinor crossed the road and walked beside the prison wall, away from the entrance from which she and Matthew had been turned away. At the opposite corner she found another way in, barred only by a long pole to keep out cars, and a notice saying: H.M. PRISON. NO ADMITTANCE.

Easy enough to duck under the pole. Pity the drive curved out of sight. She could see part of a building, a door . . . probably locked. Windows—behind which people might be sitting, looking out.

I wish I were braver, she thought. I must at least try. What can they do to me?

She looked over her shoulder and saw two men standing on the pavement, watching her.

"The entrance is down that way," one of them said, pointing.

"I was just looking."

"It's not a zoo, you know."

She flushed at the reproof in his voice, and said, "I want to see my father. They're sending me away to the country tomorrow and I want to say good-bye. But my stepmother refuses to take me and they won't let me in by myself."

"It's no good trying to sneak in the back way. You'll only get yourself into trouble," he said, but his face was now kinder than his words, encouraging her to say, though without much hope, "You wouldn't take me in, would you? You could say you were my uncle. It would only take a few minutes—"

She saw at once that she had asked the wrong people. The men exchanged amused glances, as if at a joke at her expense.

"Don't try anything like that," the first one advised her sternly. "Why won't your stepmother take you in with her? Has she seen the social worker, do you know?"

Elinor shook her head, looking uneasily from one man to the other, getting ready to run.

"Is your father a convicted prisoner or on remand?" he asked, and when Elinor did not answer, the other one said, "Has he had his trial yet?"

She shook her head dumbly.

"What's his name?"

She ran. She ran around the corner as fast as she could and scampered up the road like a hunted fox. She could hear herself panting and the sound of her feet slapping on the pavement. Nothing else. No shouts. No footsteps in pursuit. Halfway down the road she stopped and looked back. The men had not followed her.

She stood there, getting her breath back, feeling foolish. Why had she run away? Even if they were police or prison officers, they might have helped her. But she did not go back and see if they were still there. Instead she walked slowly on, stopping now and then to stand and stare up at the wall. They had run out of the cheerful sand-colored paint. That was just for show at the front where the prison faced the main road. Here the walls were blackened and grim, just as she'd always imagined a prison would look, and so high that nothing showed above them except the pale sky.

She did not know why she had come here. She hadn't really expected to find anyone willing to take her in. She just felt that she ought to have done more, though she couldn't think what. It seemed terrible that they should all go off and leave him alone.

She remembered reading that Richard I had been captured on a battlefield somewhere, and imprisoned in a dark and secret dungeon. Everybody at home had given him up for dead, except his minstrel, Blondel. Blondel had traveled from one castle to another, in sun and rain, singing outside the stone walls his master's favorite song. One day, as he paused wearily for breath, he'd heard his king's voice take up the melody, and he knew that he had found him at last. If a minstrel could do that for a moldy old king, surely a daughter could do as much for her father.

Elinor looked up at the massive walls and smiled ruefully. What was Dad's favorite song? The only one she ever remembered him singing was "Ten Green Bottles."

Regular idiot she'd sound, bellowing it at the top of her voice, when for all she knew she might be serenading the prison laundry. Fat chance Dad would hear her unless he happened to be standing just on the other side of the wall, which was hardly likely. And yet . . .

Blondel hadn't hesitated. He hadn't minded sore feet, wet clothes, and a running nose. Dogs set on him. Stones thrown. People jeering. And just for a king.

She cupped her hands around her mouth and shouted shrilly.

"Dad! Dad! It's me. Ellie. Can you hear me? Dad, it wasn't true. It wasn't true what I told Sophia! I've got it. Tell me what to do!"

Her voice scribbled uselessly against the grim wall. What an idiot I am, she thought.

"Dad! Good-bye, Dad!" she shouted.

"Is he going to be hanged?" a voice asked.

She swung around and saw two small girls looking at her with interest.

"Don't be silly, Jenny," the older one said. "They don't hang people nowadays. That's only in history."

"Why's she saying good-bye to him, then?" the younger one asked. Neither of them took their eyes off Elinor.

"Perhaps she's going away," her sister said. "He must've been a bad daddy. Only bad people go in there."

Elinor flushed with anger and opened her mouth to shout at them. But they were only babies. They hadn't meant to be rude. And it was true, she thought bitterly. He could have let her visit him. He could at least have written. He could have appealed against the decision not to grant bail, and come home to comfort Sophia when she cried at night.

"Yes, he is a bad daddy," she said with a spurt of anger. "A very bad dad indeed. I've done all I can. Now I'm going to please myself."

The next day Elinor sat in the train, looking out of the window at the fields racing by, vividly green in the sunlight and speckled with sheep. She had said good-bye to Sophia and Bambi, all kissing and crying. She had phoned Judy in Fulham, who was having a lovely time. She'd phoned Matthew in Worthing, who had sounded more guarded. Yes, he'd said, he was all right. It wasn't too bad. She'd mailed a letter to her father, giving him her new address and asking him to write to her.

She felt as free as air, all duties done and the train carrying her into a new world. She was no longer the sensible daughter, the bossy older sister, the strong one in the family. She was Elinor on her own, with only herself to please.

For the first time she wondered who Timon was, the Timon she was supposed to be company for. She hoped he was not younger than she was. She didn't want to be saddled with him. With any luck, she thought, he'd turn out to be a dog.

Chapter Ten

TIMON WAS not a dog. He was a boy of fourteen, thin, dark, with a white scar across his left cheekbone, a memento, he told her, of being stabbed in a fight in the school playground.

"Not by one of your friends, I hope," Elinor said calmly, refusing to be shocked.

He looked at her sideways. "Guess which school it was?"

"That's easy. Obviously the one Agnes has arranged for me to go to next week. Where else?" she said, and he laughed, looking suddenly quite different, almost friendly.

And that was a change indeed. When she had first come to Nettlewood, she had thought he was her enemy, like the old woman.

Agnes Carter had met her at the station and driven her through a maze of drab streets, past a concrete playground, over a bridge, and into Canal Walk, where she stopped in front of a narrow slice of a house in a gray terrace facing the canal. She'd switched off the engine and just sat there for a moment, staring at the house as if she'd never seen it before. She seemed nervous. Three times on the short journey she had said, "I hope you will be happy with us," and each time her voice had sounded more doubtful, and the hope more forlorn.

"Somebody's looking out of the window," Elinor said, seeing the net curtains twitch, and Agnes straightened up and said quickly, "Yes. What am I thinking of? Let's go in."

The house was cramped. A narrow passage was almost blocked by the bicycle leaning against the wall. Elinor followed Agnes into a small living room, so crowded with overlarge furniture that it was like an obstacle course. An old woman with a fierce beaked nose and fiercer eyes was sitting on a sofa by the window with her feet up. A thin boy with ragged dark hair was sprawling in an armchair, reading a newspaper. They stared at Elinor, but neither of them spoke. A second armchair was occupied by a large tabby-and-white cat. He, too, stared at Elinor, but she thought his expression was more friendly.

"This is Elinor, Mother," Agnes said.

"Hmph." The old lady looked Elinor up and down. "So you're that man's daughter, are you?"

"Mother!"

"Oh well, it's not her fault, I suppose," the old lady conceded, and shut her eyes.

Agnes put her hand on Elinor's shoulder, turning her hurriedly toward the boy. "And this is Timon," she said, without explaining who Timon was.

The sprawling boy, after a brief, scowling glance, muttered something inaudible and went back to his paper, leaving Elinor with a smile on her face that nobody wanted or returned.

Agnes ran her fingers through her short dark hair. "Perhaps you'll show Elinor to her room, Timon," she said, adding as an obvious bribe, "while I make us all some tea. You could carry her suitcases up for her. She must be tired."

For a moment Elinor thought the boy was going to refuse. Then, without saying anything, he threw his paper down, got to his feet, and left the room.

"Go with him, dear," Agnes said, and Elinor went quickly, keeping her eyes on the small gray case all the way up the stairs.

The attic was divided in two by a wooden partition. Half of this was to be hers. She stood looking around. It seemed unexpectedly large, possibly because there was not much furniture in it; a single bed covered with a blue-and-white quilt. A large old teddy bear sitting on a wooden chair. A white painted chest of drawers. Some daffodils in a blue vase. A dormer window framing the top branches of an apple tree.

"It's pretty," Elinor said, pleased.

From the other side of the partition came a loud belch.

"What's that?" she cried, startled.

Timon dumped her cases on the floor and turned to look at her.

"You mean Aggie didn't tell you?" he asked. "It's her brother. They shut him in there when he has one of his turns. Don't worry. He can't get at you. The door's locked. Don't take any notice if he shouts or rattles the handle. It only excites him if you answer back. Just ignore him and he'll soon get tired of it."

With that he turned and clattered down the narrow stairs, leaving Ellie looking after him. Behind the partition she heard another belch, followed by the unmistakable sound of water gurgling through unseen pipes.

So he was a joker, was he?

The door was not locked. There wasn't even a keyhole. She opened it and saw, as she had expected, that there was no one there. Only an assortment of cardboard boxes, packing cases, dented lampshades, and broken chairs; and in one corner, a water tank. She looked around thoughtfully. A possible hiding place? Plenty of choice. Behind the water tank? In one of those boxes, wrapped up in that old tablecloth? She didn't trust Timon with his odd sense of humor, his bright, noticing eyes, and his long, thin fingers. Pickpocket's hands, she thought. She'd have to find somewhere really safe to hide the stolen money.

All through supper the old woman made sniping remarks. They ate in the living room. Agnes had to pull the table away from the wall to make room for Elinor and ask Timon to fetch the stool from the kitchen for her to sit on.

"There isn't enough room," the old lady grumbled. "She's too big. Why didn't you pick the smallest if you had to have one?"

"Mother, please!" Agnes protested. She smiled uneasily at Elinor, adding, "Mother's fond of joking."

Like Timon, Elinor thought.

"I'm afraid we haven't any silver spoons for you to

eat with," Mrs. Carter said next. "These come from the garage on the corner. They give them away with the gas."

"Mother!"

"I was only making conversation. Aren't I allowed to talk? What's this you've given us? Shepherd's pie? Really, Agnes, couldn't you have given our guest something grander? I'm sure she's used to having fillet steak every night."

"Not every night," Elinor said. "Sometimes we have lobster and ostrich eggs and peacock pie."

Her attempt at a joke fell flat. The old lady sniffed, the boy stared at her, and Agnes, the only one who smiled, looked more worried than amused.

I mustn't feel sorry for her, Elinor thought, I mustn't let myself get fond of her or I'll be trapped. I don't know whether I'm going to stay here or not.

She thought of the suitcase of money, now hidden in the narrow gap between the water tank and the wall, and her head filled with dreams.

Elinor went to bed early that night. The cat followed her up to her attic room, impelled by feline curiosity to examine her possessions, sniff her bare feet, and investigate for himself the comfort of her bed. She smiled. She liked cats. And she could hear old Mrs. Carter calling him downstairs.

"Fizz! Fizz! Fizz! Where are you?"

"You stay here with me," Elinor whispered, stroking the cat. "You're too friendly to be that old witch's cat."

Someone was coming. Not Mrs. Carter. She had a bad leg and could not manage the stairs. Her bedroom was on the ground floor, next to the kitchen in what must once have been the dining room. Not Timon—the foot-steps were too light. Agnes.

Elinor picked up Fizz and pushed him through the door in the partition, shutting it behind him. Don't make a noise. Don't give me away.

She was in bed just in time. Agnes knocked on the door and came in, carrying a mug and a plate of cookies on a tray.

"I hope you like herbal tea?" she said. "It'll help you to sleep. Sometimes it's difficult to get to sleep in a new place, especially when there's a full moon. I meant to make some curtains for your window, but I'm afraid I never got around to it."

"It doesn't matter. I like looking out."

Agnes moved the teddy bear off the chair and put the tray in its place.

"I hope you like the tea," she said again. "Timon hates it. He says it's like pond water."

"Who is Timon?" Elinor asked. "I mean, is he a relative? I'm afraid I don't know much about our family," she added, seeing Agnes look at her in surprise.

"Didn't your father tell you? No, I suppose he wouldn't. He wasn't really interested. Sometimes I don't think he ever listened—" She broke off and bent down to pick the teddy bear off the floor.

"He was always busy," Elinor said.

"Yes. Yes, of course. He must've had a lot on his mind." Agnes sat down on the foot of the bed with the teddy bear on her lap and looked down at it. "He used to be mine," she said. "This bear, I mean, not Timon. Though Timon is an old friend too. Part of the family now." She hesitated and for a moment Elinor thought she was going to leave it like that, but then she went on slowly, "He came to live with my parents about six years ago. They had a house in Nettley then. They were rather old to be foster parents, I suppose, but my mother was set on it, and she's good at getting her own way. I expect she was lonely. I had already left home and come to live here."

"Didn't you visit them?"

"Yes, of course. Several times a week. Nettley is only five miles away. But it's not the same as having someone in the house. Someone young. Mother always wanted a boy."

"Did you mind?"

"Mind? No. Why should I mind?" Agnes said, flushing a little. "Timon's a good boy. He was very kind to Mother when my father died. I don't know how we'd have managed without him. I came down with the flu. I couldn't do as much as I wanted. Timon looked after everything."

"Doesn't he have any family?" Elinor asked. "Of his own, I mean?"

"He didn't get on with his stepfather. There were difficulties. . . . I don't know the whole story. He hardly tells me anything. It's my mother you want to ask. She's in his confidence, not me," Agnes said, and then added quickly, "No. You'd better not ask her. She wouldn't tell you; she likes secrets. Not that there's any mystery about Timon, you mustn't think that. He had an unhappy childhood and doesn't like to talk about it, that's all. So please don't ask him about it, will you, Elinor?"

Before Elinor could answer, they heard Mrs. Carter,

calling her cat again. She was out in her garden, and her voice came up through the branches of the apple tree, old and cracked.

"Fizz! Fizz! Fizz!"

"That's Mother," Agnes said unnecessarily. "She likes Fizz to be in at night. She often can't sleep and he's company for her." She glanced at Elinor and added, "Her leg's been very painful today. It makes her a little irritable. You mustn't mind. We're all very glad to have you here."

With that she bent down and kissed Elinor good-night, and then left the room. Elinor listened to her footsteps pattering down the stairs. Then she got up and let the cat out of the other half of the attic. She tried to shoo him down the stairs, but he dodged past her and ran under the bed.

Elinor shrugged and walked over to the window. The sense of freedom she had felt on the train was slipping away. And yet, she thought, I could buy a ticket to anywhere in the world. I could take Matt and Judy with me. We could set off tomorrow and never come back. Let them whistle for us.

The apple blossom gleamed pale against the dark sky. Behind it she could see the somber hump of the woods. A breath of air, damp and sweet, blew across her face.

Money was not enough. They'd need passports. She sighed.

The cat jumped onto the windowsill beside her and, before she could stop him, leapt onto the branch of the apple tree, which bounced wildly beneath his weight. He crouched there for a moment, surveying the night with an air of proud ownership. Then he vanished with a rustle of leaves into the depths of the tree. She looked after him, wishing with all her heart she could be as bold and unfettered as he was.

Chapter Eleven

ELINOR DREAMED of the prison that night. The massive wall was black in the moonlight. She climbed the ladder that rested against it, a long whippy ladder that bounced at every step, going up and up into the windy sky. She had no fear of falling. When she reached the top, she looked down and saw her father standing on the other side.

"There you are, Ellie," he said, looking up at her and smiling. "Come and have tea."

She tried to jump down but could not move her legs. Something heavy weighed them down. "I can't," she said, and opened her eyes.

She was back in her attic room. The cat had returned and was lying on her feet, fast asleep. She lay looking out of the window at the branch of the apple tree, blowing in the wind. She wondered if her father was lying awake, too, and what he could see from his window. No apple tree. Slices of sky between the bars. She ought to have given the money to Sophia. Perhaps Sophia could have bribed someone, arranged an escape, like in her dream, a ladder against the wall. . . . Or perhaps Sophia would have gone off with it and never come back.

It was too late now.

The moon was very bright and it made her restless. She was thirsty, that was the trouble. She hadn't liked the herbal tea Agnes had given her and had poured it out of the window before going to bed. If she went down to the kitchen and helped herself to milk out of the fridge, would they call that stealing? Would they say she took after her father?

She moved her feet carefully, but the cat woke up and ran ahead of her out of the attic and down the narrow stairs. When she reached the landing, she stopped in surprise. There were noises coming from below. Voices talking. Laughter. Now someone was singing. The cat had vanished.

She crept down the next flight of stairs. Mrs. Carter's door was open. A small light shone down onto the empty bed, its covers half dragged off onto the floor behind it. On the bedside table a radio babbled softly, among a crowd of medicine bottles, a cookie jar, two glasses of water (one containing false teeth), three paperbacks, spectacles, and a small enameled box. The rest of the room was in deep shadow.

Where was the old lady?

As Elinor hesitated, she heard a faint scrabbling sound coming from the floor on the other side of the bed, as if someone was lying there, trying to pull herself up. She ran into the room and saw something move out of the darkness toward her, the glimmer of a disembodied face, floating in the air like a pale balloon. She cried out and backed away, and the face, too, retreated, as if equally afraid.

There was the sound of footsteps in the passage, and a voice said, "Who's there? Oh, it's you. What are you doing in my room?"

Elinor turned. Mrs. Carter was standing in the doorway. Her feet were bare and her long white nightie flapped loosely around her thin old body like the sail of a stranded ship. She looked older and more frail without her teeth, but there was nothing weak about her anger.

"What are you doing here? How dare you come into my room! Am I to have no privacy? What do you want?"

"There's something there!"

"Where? What are you talking about? I can't see anything."

"A face, look!" But even as she pointed, Elinor realized her mistake. For the ghostly face had company now. A pale smudge of a figure was standing beside it, the white nightie showing where her own navy dressing-gown had been invisible.

"It's a mirror, you stupid girl," Mrs. Carter said coldly.

"Oh."

"What were you doing in my room? You'd no right to be in here at all."

"I—I thought you'd fallen out of bed."

"Really? You woke up in the middle of the night and thought you'd better come downstairs and see if I'd fallen out of bed? Is that what you're asking me to believe? You must think I'm very simple." Mrs. Carter looked around the room and added sharply, "Where's my watch? I left it on the table. I know I did. You've stolen it, you horrid girl!"

"I haven't!" Elinor shouted. "I haven't touched it!"

"What's that you've got in your hand?"

"Nothing." Elinor unclenched her fingers and held out her hands palms upward. "Nothing."

"Your pockets, then. Turn out your pockets."

Neither of them heard the soft footsteps on the stairs. A knock on the door made them jump and swing around. Timon was standing in the doorway, a coat over his pajamas, his hair tousled. His eyes looked bright and wide awake. "Can anyone join in?" he asked.

"Timon, she's taken my watch. My silver watch," Mrs. Carter said. "I left it on the table as I always do. Here." She went over and tapped the edge of the table nearest the bed. "That's where it—" She broke off, and her crumpled old face turned pink.

"What is it? Is it there? Come on, Ma, own up," Timon said gently. He sounded fond of the old woman. "Anyone can make a mistake," he said.

"Must've fallen off," Mrs. Carter mumbled. Reaching out her hand, she brought up a silver wristwatch out of the tumbled pillows. "Never did that before." She darted a resentful glance at Elinor as if it was all her fault, and muttered, "I'm sorry. I was wrong, it seems."

Elinor was too angry to appreciate the effort this apology had cost the old lady. She said in a high, clear voice, "I came into your room because I heard a noise behind your bed and thought you might've fallen and hurt yourself. I won't bother next time."

"Oh, go away. I'm tired," Mrs. Carter said, sitting down on the bed. "I'm too old for all this. Tell her to go away, Timon."

"I'm going!" Elinor said, and ran out of the room. Too

angry to think where she was going, she turned right instead of left and found herself in the kitchen. Moonlight, coming through the window, showed her the pale oblong of the fridge. She had wanted some milk, she remembered. She hesitated, looking back down the passage. Light from the open doorway patterned the carpet. She heard Timon say, "Now you'll be able to sleep, Ma. Good night."

He shut the door behind him and immediately vanished into darkness, but he must have seen her silhouetted against the moonlit kitchen because he said, "Why don't you put on the light?"

She did so and saw him coming toward her.

"You're not going to run away in your dressing gown," he said. "So what are you doing down here?"

"I was thirsty," she said.

"You can't have milk," he said promptly. "Or there won't be enough for breakfast. You can have tea."

"Thanks."

He filled the kettle and switched it on. "Next time do it yourself," he said. "The tea bags are kept in here. Spoon in that drawer. Do you take sugar?"

"No."

"Good. Nor do I. You know that noise you said you heard? It was her cat, Fizz. He was lying on the blankets on the floor. Dunno where he came from. He wasn't in her room last night. We searched everywhere. Didn't you hear us calling?"

"Yes," she said, leaning against a cupboard. There was nowhere to sit down.

"You had him!" Timon said, guessing. "You had him in your room all the time we were calling."

"I didn't do it on purpose. He followed me up there. How was I to know he was her cat? He was friendly—"

"And she isn't? What did you expect?" he asked, staring at her curiously. "I couldn't believe it when I heard you were coming here. I thought Aggie must've gone mad. Unless—perhaps she got tired of having us, crowding her, getting in her way. Maybe she hoped you'd drive us out, me and Ma."

"I don't understand. Why should I drive you out? She hates me, doesn't she, the old lady? Why, what have I done?"

"Nothing," he admitted. "Nothing at all. But like it says in the Bible, the sins of the father shall be visited on the children, something like that. I always thought it was unfair."

So that was it. The old crow thought she and her father had brought disgrace on the family. She was afraid the neighbors would get to know, that Elinor would tell someone at school and it would get around the small town. . . .

"You needn't worry," she said, her voice shaking with anger. "I'm not staying here. I'm leaving. First thing tomorrow, I'm off."

"She was just cross," he said, catching hold of her arm. "She didn't really think you'd clipped her watch, she didn't think at all. She'll be sorry when she wakes up and remembers."

But Elinor pulled away from him and ran upstairs to her attic room, slamming the door behind her.

Elinor opened her eyes and lay for a time, staring out of the window and thinking. The sky was the wrong shape.

She was in a strange bed in a strange house in an unfamiliar town, that was why. Behind the partition a water tank belched and gurgled. Someone somewhere had turned on a tap. It was morning. She got up, put on her dressing gown, and went out onto the small landing.

Timon was sitting at the top of the narrow stairs, his back leaning against one wall, his feet pressed against the other, blocking her way.

"You forgot your tea last night," he said, getting to his feet and picking up a mug from the floor. "So I brought you some more. About ten minutes ago, so it won't be very hot. You're a heavy sleeper, aren't you? I knocked several times."

"I didn't hear you. The water tank was making such a noise."

"That was Aggie taking her bath. She's gone down to make breakfast now. Bacon and eggs on Sundays," he told her. He was gazing over her shoulder into her room, his eyes going backward and forward as if searching for something.

"What are you looking for?" she asked.

"Nothing. Just looking. You haven't got Fizz in there again?"

"No."

"Mind if I look under the bed?" Before she could answer, he pushed past her into her room, knelt down, and peered under her bed. "No," he said. "No cat. Only a suitcase." He got to his feet again. "Where is the other one?" he asked. "You had two, this one and a small one. I carried them up for you."

Her heart began thumping, but she answered without hesitation, giving the lie she had prepared, not really thinking she'd need it. "I put it in the big one to make room. Why?"

"I just wondered," he said, shrugging. He moved about the room, glancing at her clothes hanging from the row of hooks on the partition wall and then at the small chest of drawers. "Got enough space for your things?" he asked, and began pulling open the drawers.

"What are you doing?" she demanded.

"Nothing. Just playing the host. Asking if you're comfortable and all that," he said, edging toward the door. She stretched out her hand and slammed it shut.

"Now you can tell me what you were really looking for," she said. "Don't say it was Fizz. I'm not stupid. I bet he's still asleep on her bed. What's she lost this time? A pearl necklace? The family silver? Her pension book?"

"Calm down. You don't want to be paranoid about what happened last night. She was just cross. Now open that door and don't ever try to shut me in again," he said, suddenly looking dangerous.

She opened the door and let him out.

"That's better," he said. "As a matter of fact, I was only looking to see if you'd packed your clothes yet. You said you were leaving. First thing in the morning you'd be off, you said."

"I've changed my mind," she told him. "I'm staying. Sorry."

She expected this news to anger him. Instead he looked—she couldn't decide what the expression on his face was. Relieved? Pleased? Amused?

"Then I'd better tell Aggie to fry some bacon and eggs for you," he said, and went clattering down the stairs.

She looked after him thoughtfully. Then she went into

the other half of the attic, picking her way carefully over the broken lampshades and rolls of carpet, and peered into the dark, narrow gap between the water tank and the wall. The small suitcase was still there; she could just make it out. Looking around, she selected a piece of black cloth from one of the boxes and pushed it into the gap so that the outlines of the case were hidden. Then very carefully with her fingers, she detached a large, thick cobweb from a corner in the rafters and draped it across the cloth. A spider let itself down on a gossamer thread and hurried out of sight.

I'd make a good criminal, she thought. Better than Dad.

Chapter Twelve

IF OLD Mrs. Carter was sorry when she woke up and remembered the night before, she did not say so to Elinor. She sat down to lunch without a word to anyone, unless a grunt could be taken as a greeting of some sort. Elinor thought she looked more like an old crow than ever, hunched over her food with her fierce eyes hooded.

They were having lunch early because Agnes and Mrs. Carter were going over to Nettley in the afternoon. "We go there every Sunday," Agnes said. "Mother misses her friends and it's the only chance she has of seeing them. You're very welcome to come with us, Elinor."

"She wouldn't like it," the old lady said flatly. "She'd be bored. Why should she want to spend her time with a lot of old women?"

"I'm not old yet, thank you," Agnes said with a show of spirit.

"Old enough to be her mother." Mrs. Carter turned to Elinor and added, "You wouldn't like to tag along with your mother everywhere she went, would you?"

"Yes, I would," Elinor retorted, simply to contradict

the old woman. But suddenly an old memory came vividly into her mind. She was a small child again, crying, "Wait for me! Wait for me!" and her mother had turned and held out her arms. . . . To her embarrassment Elinor's eyes filled with tears and she looked quickly down at her plate to hide them. There was a short silence. Then the old lady mumbled, "Sorry."

Elinor could not answer. She was furious with herself. She couldn't bear to cry in front of her enemy. She stuffed some roast chicken into her mouth and chewed it fiercely, willing the tears away, concentrating so hard on this that she did not hear what they were saying. When she looked up at last she was surprised to find they were all smiling at her, even the old lady.

"You'd like that, wouldn't you, Elinor?" Agnes said.

Elinor had no idea what she was talking about. Rather than admit this, it seemed simpler to say, "Yes." It was only at the end of the meal that she discovered that she'd agreed to go out with Timon that afternoon, he on the bicycle he kept in the narrow hall and she on an old one belonging to Agnes, that lived in the garden shed along with the spiders and the wood lice.

"It may not be up to much, but the brakes work," he told her, wheeling it out into the road. "You can ride a bicycle, I hope?"

"Yes."

"You don't sound very certain. How long is it since you rode one?"

"Oh, a few years. Four or five. But they say you never forget."

"We'll start off on the towpath," he decided. "I'd rather you fell into the canal than under a car. Aggie will blame me if I don't bring you back alive. When I consider you roadworthy, I'll show you the sights of Nettlewood; the school, the brewery, the town dump, the gasworks, and any other place I think might interest you."

"Like the railway station?"

He looked at her sharply. "You're not really thinking of leaving, are you?"

"No, I'm not," she said. "How can I resist a town with so many attractions?"

"I thought you'd find it difficult," he said, but she thought he looked relieved, as if for some reason it was important that she stay in Nettlewood.

Timon spent not only Sunday afternoon, but most of the next two days with her, though he went out every evening by himself and did not come back till late. At first she wondered if he was a solitary person without friends, but this was not so. Often as they cycled through the town, boys would call out greetings; "Hey, Timon, where are you off to?" "Stop a minute!" "Who's your girlfriend?"

He never stopped. He just smiled and held up his hand, in a gesture half like a salute, half like a warning: Stop where you are. Don't follow us.

As they rode on, she'd turn in her saddle and see the boys staring after them.

"If you keep doing that, you'll fall off," Timon told her.

"They're waving. I think they want to talk to you."

"They can wait. I'm seeing them tonight."

He doesn't want them to meet me, she thought, and wondered why not. He wasn't really her friend, she must remember that.

But it was difficult to think of Timon as an enemy. The

sun was shining and the town was not as unattractive as she'd first thought. There was a main street with all the familiar shops, Boots and Woolworth's and Marks and Spencer's. There was a market square with a fountain in the middle, and tubs of flowers and parked cars. There was a church with a tall spire, and a bridge where they stopped for a moment to look down at the painted barges on the canal.

"Narrow boats, they call them," Timon told her. "People live in the one at the end all the year round. It must be cold in winter when the canal freezes over. Aggie says she used to skate on it when she was a girl, but I guess winters were different then. Last year the ice was so thin, it melted if you breathed on it. Come on, I'll take you to see the school, so you'll know your way on Wednesday."

Nettlewood Junior High was on the edge of the town, a low modern building, with glass windows glinting in the sun. The playground was empty and quiet. There was grass and small trees and flowers in the neat beds.

"It looks peaceful," Elinor said.

"Wait till Wednesday."

"Of course. I forgot. This is where you got your scar in a knife fight."

He grinned. "I made that up," he admitted. "Like Aggie's mad brother in the attic. I was afraid you'd find Nettlewood too dull for you after London."

"How did you get your scar, then?" she asked curiously, and saw at once that this was one of the forbidden questions. "He doesn't like to talk about it," Agnes had told her. His face became bleak and angry. She said quickly, looking away from him, "I expect you fell off your bike."

"My stepfather hit me," Timon said. "He was always hitting me. That's why I ran away. Didn't Aggie tell you?"

"She just said that you didn't get on together very well."

"Dear Aggie," Timon said, with a scornful laugh. "She's as soft as butter. She's afraid to talk to me about it in case I burst into tears. She forgets I'm no longer seven years old. It doesn't upset me to talk about it now, it just bores me."

But it did upset him still. Elinor could see the tightness in his face. This wasn't another of his stories. This was true.

"It bores me to talk about Dad," she said. "About his being in prison, I mean. People ask so many questions and you have to keep saying the same thing over and over again, don't you?"

"No, you don't," he said, his face suddenly relaxing into a smile. "You can tell them different things each time like I do. I was the scourge of the social workers. They never knew what to believe. You could say your father was a patient in a leper colony. Or had been kidnapped by brigands in Turkey, and you were saving up to pay the ransom. Or he'd run away with a snake charmer. There're hundreds of stories you could tell."

"But it wouldn't do any good, would it?" she asked. "They know about Dad already. I saw the way they stared at me when we went past."

"People who wear bright pink trousers must expect to be stared at," he said lightly, and started cycling back the way they had come.

But it hadn't been that sort of look, she thought as she followed him. She knew what it was. Curiosity. She'd seen it in the eyes of their neighbors after Dad had been arrested. People who'd never bothered to return her smile, now stopped and asked, "How are you, dear. It must have been terrible for you all. . . ." Even the dog at Number 6, who'd always ignored her before, had hurled itself against its garden gate and started barking hysterically, as if she'd suddenly grown horns.

They stopped at the Singing Kettle in the marketplace for tea, and as they followed the waitress to a small table in the center of the crowded room, she watched the people at the other tables. Some glanced at them idly, without interest. Some did not even look up. But at one table, a woman nudged her companion and they both stared at Elinor. Though they looked away when she glared back, she seemed to feel their glances clinging to her skin like cobwebs.

"There!" she said, as they sat down. "Did you see?"

"See what?"

"Those two women. Did you see the way they looked at me? Not at my trousers—there're plenty of people wearing pink trousers, even in Nettlewood. They'd heard. I know they had. Someone told them about Dad."

"Not me," Timon said promptly.

"Who, then? No, don't bother to tell me. I can guess."

He shook his head. "If you mean Ma, you're wrong. More likely to be Aggie. You may find it difficult to believe, but Nettlewood is a popular school, always full to the brim. You're lucky you don't have to go to one of the dumps at Nettley. I expect Aggie had to tell them the sad tale to get you in—what's the matter? You've gone as red as a fire engine."

"She had no right to," Elinor said, her voice shaking with anger. "I don't want anybody's pity, thank you."

"Don't you?" he asked, sounding surprised. "I don't see why not. It never worried me. In fact it came in very useful at times. Got me out of trouble more than once. You wouldn't have liked those schools in Nettley, take my word for it."

"I don't need pity," she said stiffly. "I can look after myself. I'm strong."

"Strong!" he exclaimed, hooting with laughter. "You strong? You've been wrapped up in money so long—" He broke off. The waitress had come to their table and, hearing this last remark, was looking with interest at Elinor's jacket, as if wondering how much it had cost. Timon ordered two cream teas and, when the waitress had gone, went on, "You don't know what it's like out in the world. You're liable to catch cold if you're not careful. Even Ma is sorry for you. That's why she asked me to keep an eye on you till we're back at school."

"What!"

"Yeah. She was afraid you'd do some fool thing like running off. You wouldn't do anything so stupid, would you? It's a sure way to end up dead in a ditch."

"Mrs. Carter asked you to look after me?"

"Yeah. I just said."

"How much is she paying you?"

"Ten pounds," he said, grinning at her. "But I've got to pay for our cream teas out of that. Tomorrow we'll take sandwiches or I'll be out of pocket. You're not going to sulk and refuse to come, are you? After all, you haven't even seen the sewage plant and the town dump yet. I was saving them up."

She gave a grudging smile, trying to hide the fact that she was deeply offended. "Oh, I might as well come," she said. "Why not? I don't care what made you take me out."

"That's better," he said approvingly. "Now you're learning. Being strong has nothing to do with pride. If you're strong, you don't care what people think of you."

Don't you? she wondered, as the waitress brought their tea. Not even people you love?

But she did not say this aloud. She had a feeling Timon would think love made you soft—and perhaps he was right. But being strong didn't seem to have made him happy. His face, as he looked down at the scone he was cutting, was as thin and sad as a stray cat's.

"Have some cream," she said, pushing the bowl toward him.

He looked up and smiled at her.

"I've decided to leave the sewage plant till Tuesday," he told her. "Tomorrow I'll take you to Stinging Nettle Cottage. Wear something warm, it'll be cold. It's always cold there. Perhaps we'll be lucky and see the woman with a white face."

"Who's she?" Elinor asked, but he laughed and wouldn't tell her.

After supper that evening Elinor, bored with watching television, went to fetch a book from her room. The hall light was on but the landing above was in shadow. When she was halfway up the stairs, she heard, to her astonishment, soft noises, like footsteps coming stealthily down the wooden steps from the attic.

"Fizz?" she called, her heart beating fast. "Is that you, Fizz?"

The landing light went on and she saw it was Timon.

"I thought you'd gone out. You said you were going out!" she said.

"So I am." He smiled at her, obviously feeling no need to explain what he'd been doing. Perhaps she'd mistaken the sounds. He might have been walking about in his room, or coming back from the bathroom—in the dark? Why not? His eyes were as bright as a cat's, he could probably see in the dark.

Looking over the banister, she watched him run down the stairs. He turned at the front door to look back at her. "Good night," he said, and waved his hand. That was a mistake: she'd never have noticed otherwise how dirty it was, the thin fingers gray as dust.

When he had gone, she raced up to the attic and, kneeling down in front of the water tank, thrust her arm into the dark narrow gap between the tank and the wall. The small case was there, still covered with the black cloth she had wrapped around it to disguise its outlines.

She sat back on her heels and smiled with relief. She was getting nervous, seeing thieves everywhere, suspecting Timon just because his hands were dirty. Boys, after all, are hardly famous for cleanliness. And there was no reason why he should suspect that she had anything to hide.

She did not notice, as she got to her feet and went back to her room, that there was a clear handprint in the dust on the floor by the water tank, the print of a larger hand than hers, thin, with long fingers.

Chapter Thirteen

SPRING WAS late. The trees in the wood had only just come out in a rash of tiny leaves, speckling the gray sky. Timon and Elinor wheeled their bicycles along a narrow track, too rough and littered with fallen twigs and branches for them to ride over. Holly bushes leaned out to catch at them as they went by, and at last their way was blocked by a fallen oak, its dead and leafless branches forming a wooden barricade impossible to shift.

"What do we do now?" Elinor asked.

"Hide our bikes behind the holly, climb over the trees, and walk. It's not far now."

"Somebody might steal them."

"We'll put on padlocks, if you like," he said. "But I've been here often and never met anyone. Nobody ever comes this way."

Elinor didn't blame them. She was used to London woods, with neat paths and a playing field in the middle, and a café where you could buy ice cream in summer. She found these wild, matted woods a little sinister, the trees crowding too close, the overgrown holly darkening the day. What was she doing here, following a strange boy who might, for all he now seemed friendly, still be her enemy?

"Does anyone live in the cottage?" she asked.

"Hardly ever."

"What about the woman with a white face?"

"They say she visits occasionally."

"At midnight, I suppose," she said suspiciously. "When the moon's full and bats are about."

He laughed and agreed that was the general idea. "She's been dead over fifty years," he told her.

"Then I'm not surprised she's got a white face," Elinor said.

"You're a funny girl. Doesn't anything scare you?" he asked.

"Plenty," she said, but she was pleased by the admiration in his voice. He's beginning to like me, she thought. Give him a few more days and I'll win him over. He'll be on my side and his horrible old ma had better look out.

The holly was thicker here. Timon walked ahead, stopping occasionally to hold back branches so they would not whip into her face. They came to a place where the branches interlaced to form a barrier of fanged leaves, and they had to crawl on their hands and knees until they came out into a clearing.

"I hope it's going to be worth seeing," she said.

"Judge for yourself."

He stepped aside, and she saw a small stone house, almost black with damp and streaked with a sick green mold. It had a front door in the middle and a barred window on either side, the bars red with rust. On the floor above were three small, shuttered windows. It looked like a child's drawing of a prison—except most children would have put sad faces at the windows and hands reaching out through the bars—at least, she would have.

She didn't say anything and Timon was silent, too, watching her face. Then he turned and led his way across the patch of waste ground that must once have been a garden. It was ankle high in stinging nettles. She was glad she had worn trousers and socks.

"In summer they come up above your waist," he told her. "It's like wading through a stinging sea. You can feel them reaching up for your face and you're frightened of tripping. You must come here in summer."

"No, thank you."

They reached the cottage and he put out his hand toward the door.

"Isn't it locked?" she asked.

"I've got the key," he said. "I found it under that second flowerpot when I first came here. That's where people leave their spare keys, under flowerpots or doormats or up on high ledges. That's where you want to look." He unlocked the door and did not notice the doubtful glance she gave him.

"I don't want to go inside."

"What's the matter?" he asked, turning to look at her. "You don't really believe in ghosts, do you?"

"Of course not."

"Then what are you frightened of? Me?"

"Don't be stupid," she said, flushing.

He laughed, opened the front door wide, stepped back, and waved her in.

"Come into my parlor, said the spider to the fly."

He was mocking her. She should never have come into the woods with him at all. What did she really know about this thin, bright-eyed boy and his horrible old foster ma? The door had opened too easily. Noiselessly. The hinges had been oiled. Terrible things did happen. She'd read about them in the papers, seen them on the news. What had made her think that they could never happen to her?

She could have tried to escape, to have pushed past him and fled for her life, but she didn't. She was too embarrassed to run away. She could be wrong, and then he'd never let her forget it. It'd be all over the school. Agnes would think she was mad. . . .

So she walked through the front door—and heard it slam shut behind her, and the sound of the key turning in the lock.

Oh God, no!

There was nobody behind her. He hadn't followed her. He'd slammed the door shut and locked her in. Why?

She stood still, trying to control her rapid, ragged breathing, letting her eyes get accustomed to the dim light. She was in a narrow windowless passage. A door on her left was half open, letting in some gray, dusty daylight. A narrow flight of stairs led steeply up and disappeared around a dark corner.

"Elinor! Elinor! Come to the window! I have to talk to you!"

She heard Timon plainly but did not answer. Instead she walked quickly down the passage and found herself in a small square kitchen, with a cold stone floor and a chipped white enamel sink below a small barred window. There was no back door.

"Elinor! Come to the window! Come and talk!"

"Shut up!" she muttered under her breath, and went back down the passage. She looked for a moment at the half-open door, but then turned away and put her hand on the banister.

"Don't try and go upstairs!" Timon shouted. "They're not safe. The floors are rotten!"

She looked around sharply. Could he see her? No, there was no way. No mail slot in the front door. No crack wide enough to peer through. He must have heard the floorboards creak beneath her weight, and guessed where she was. Defiantly she started up the stairs, keeping close to the wall. The old wood complained at every step as she climbed up into the dark. There were no doors open here and she was close to panic, fearing there might be gaping holes in the floor she could not see. For a moment she was too frightened to move, then she forced herself to slide her feet carefully forward, inch by anxious inch, moving her hands over the passage wall until they came to a door, a handle—

The light seemed almost dazzling, even though the unshuttered window was small and very dirty. She was in a room at the back of the house. Going over to the window and looking down, she could see another patch of waste ground, a dark pond at the far end, around which the trees were crowding, and some sort of ditch or stream. There was no sign of a road or other houses, only trees, trees everywhere.

She was about to turn from the window when she saw Timon come around the corner of the house. He did not look up but walked along until he was immediately below her and then came so close to the house that she could no longer see him, even though she pressed her nose against the dirty pane. It was a sash window and looked as if it hadn't been opened for a hundred years. The catch, as she'd expected, refused to move.

Timon stepped back from the house, looked up, and saw her.

"So there you are!" he shouted. "Come downstairs. I want to talk to you."

She did not answer.

He waited a moment, then shrugged his shoulders and walked back around the corner of the house, out of sight.

Elinor waited by the window, not knowing what to do. Five minutes passed and he did not come back. She went out of the room, leaving the door open to give some light, and tried the doors on the other side. Both rooms were unlocked and dark, their windows closed and shuttered. She hesitated, then went slowly and carefully downstairs and through the open door on the left.

The room was empty, except for dust, and old yellow newspapers scattered over the floor. It was colder in here. There was no glass in the window. She crossed the room quietly and looked through the bars.

Timon was sitting comfortably on a low branch of a tree, eating their sandwiches.

She watched him for a moment, feeling angry and bewildered, but no longer frightened. He looked younger with his mouth full of cheese and tomato, and crumbs all over his jacket. It was probably some stupid joke.

"All right," she called. "You can talk to me. I don't promise I'll listen."

He looked around and let himself drop to the ground. Even when he'd swallowed his mouthful, he did not smile but came through the nettles and stood in front of her, just too far away for her to reach him through the bars, had she wanted to hit him.

"You'd better get this straight right away," he told her. "There's no way out of there. The bars may be rusty, but they're firm. I know. I tried them. The door's locked and I've got the only key. You can scream if you like. Nobody will hear you. Go on. Try."

He did not expect her to do so, so she did. It was oddly difficult. She opened her mouth and a thin, self-conscious squeal came out. She tried again and this time it came louder and louder. When she stopped, it was still ringing through the woods, bouncing from tree to tree. Birds flew up, applauding with their wings. A small squirrel froze on a branch. They waited, but nobody came.

"Right," Timon said briskly. "Now we've got that sorted out, let's talk business. I'm not going to let you out of there, not today, not tomorrow, not ever, unless you agree to my terms."

"What terms?"

"I want the money. The money your dad stole from Ma. I want it back," he said.

Chapter Fourteen

"I DON'T know what you mean," Elinor said, turning as red as a plum.

He meant fifty thousand pounds, he told her, a little over, in fact, but her dad could keep the change. Ma wasn't greedy. She just wanted her savings back, the money Elinor's dad had cheated her out of, persuading her to invest it in his rotten company, promising all sorts of advantages and all the time meaning to sneak off to South America with it. Only, the police had got him first, good for them.

"I don't know what you mean," she said again, her heart thumping. She was not a good liar. Even in her own ears her voice sounded unconvincing.

So that was why old Mrs. Carter hated her, not only because of the disgrace of Dad's being in prison, but because he had stolen her savings. I should've guessed, Elinor thought. But how could he have done it to one of his own family? A boring lot, he'd called them, but not so boring, apparently, when they had money to lose.

"It's not true! It can't be!" she cried, raising her voice to try and drown out these bitter thoughts. "When could he have done it? He hasn't seen any of you for years. He'd no chance. Besides," she added belatedly, "he wouldn't do such a thing. He hasn't been found guilty yet. You talk as if . . ." Her voice shook and she broke off, putting her hand over her mouth.

"Oh, don't put on an act," he said impatiently, though she hadn't been. She was genuinely upset, more upset than she could have expected, to find her father had cheated the old woman out of her savings. It turned Mrs. Carter from an ogre into a victim, a poor old lady whose bad leg kept her awake at night with only her cat for company, and the radio babbling, the false teeth grinning in the glass, and three paperbacks on her bedside table to keep the shadows away. There'd be no fun fighting her anymore.

"It's no good playing the innocent," Timon went on. "You're in it with him, aren't you? You're a kind of thief too. He gave it to you, didn't he? Or some of it."

"Some of it?"

"The money. The loot. It's in the small case, isn't it?"

"The small case?"

"Are you a lousy parrot? The case. The small case! The one I carried up to the attic for you, the one you looked like you wanted to snatch away from me in case I made off with it, the one you couldn't take your eyes off. That small case. Your face is very expressive, did you know that? You want to watch it. I found it yesterday— you nearly caught me, remember? It's behind the water tank in the attic. The most obvious place—you're not a very good criminal, are you? No wonder your dad was caught, if he takes after you. Still," he added generously, "you did put a dark cloth in front to make it difficult to see, and a most artistic cobweb. I suppose it might have fooled some people."

"But not you."

"No, not me."

All the time he'd been talking, she'd been trying to think what to do, but her mind felt blank and stupid. It's just the shock, she thought, the shock of being found out. That must be how Dad felt, that must be why he's shutting himself away from us. I wouldn't mind a prison cell to hide in right now—

She saw her hands holding the bars of the window and realized she was in a sort of prison. She didn't have to go on talking to Timon. She could go and hide in one of the upstairs rooms with the shuttered windows. . . . Then she remembered Timon had the key to the front door.

"I don't understand," she said. "Why have you shut me in here? You've got the case. Why don't you just make off with it? You said something about agreeing to your terms. What terms? What do you want now?"

"The key," he said.

"The key?"

"Stop repeating everything I say!" he shouted, suddenly losing his temper. "The key! The key! Are you deaf?"

"But you've got it." He looked at her blankly, so she added, "You locked me in. I heard the key turn. Don't say you've gone and lost it!"

It was, of course, a misunderstanding. He called her stupid and she said he was. How could she have guessed he meant the key to the little case? Even her brother Matthew, who was only nine, had offered to force the locks for her. She could have done it herself with a pen-knife, if she'd wanted to.

"Don't tell me you didn't want to damage the case," she said scornfully. "You didn't think twice about stealing it."

"That's just the point," he said. "I can't steal it. I promised Ma on my honor that I'd never steal again. That's why you've got to give me the key. She wouldn't touch the money if she thought I'd stolen it, even though it's rightfully hers. But if you give me the key, it'd be different."

Elinor stared at him. She had thought he was clever, for some reason she couldn't now remember. Perhaps the brightness of his eyes had misled her. But even Matthew wouldn't have concocted such a silly scheme. Even Judy would have had more sense.

"You mean she won't mind your locking me up in this horrible house, without food—or water from the look of that rusty tap in the kitchen? She won't mind your threatening not to let me out until I give you the key? You did say that, didn't you? Not today, not tomorrow, not ever, isn't that what you said?"

"Yeah. That's right," he agreed.

"And you really don't think she'd mind that?"

"Why should she? I only promised not to steal. I never said anything about kidnapping or extortion."

She laughed. She could not believe he was serious. "Come on, Timon, let me out," she said. "I can take a joke, but I'm cold and hungry now. Let me out."

He shook his head. "You'd better believe me. I mean it. Give me the key."

"I haven't got the key."

"You're lying. It's no good. I can tell. It's on that chain around your neck, I'd bet a hundred pounds—"

"Then you'd lose it." She pulled the thin gold chain up from under her sweatshirt and showed him there was nothing on it. He stared at it angrily.

"Why do you wear it under your clothes, then?" he asked, as if he thought she'd fooled him on purpose.

"I don't know. Just do," she said, shrugging. "Less swanky, I suppose. Less likely to be snatched."

"God!" he said, staring at her. "What a life you lead. Hiding your money behind the water tank and your gold under your shirt—I wonder you can sleep at night. But you can't, can you? You go prowling down to the kitchen. Why don't you give me the key and let me take the case? It would be one weight off your mind."

It would be at that, she thought. He could have the gold chain, too, for all she cared.

"I'd give you the key if I had it, but I haven't," she said. "I never had it. I don't know what's in the case."

"You're lying again," he said, not wanting to believe her. She was relieved to find that he could not really tell.

He made her turn out her pockets and pass him her purse and crumpled hanky through the bars so that he could examine them for hidden keys. She began to feel humiliated and so angry that she could not speak. There was an opened letter from Annabel in one of the pockets of her jacket and when he told her to hand it over, she refused, for no better reason than to defy him.

"No!" she shouted. "I won't! I've had enough of you!"

He was silent for a moment. Then he shrugged and said coldly, "All right. I'll give you till tomorrow to think better of it."

With that he walked away, turning to look back when he reached the holly and shout, "If you hear noises, it'll only be the rats." Then he ducked down and crawled under the low branches until he was out of sight.

"They'll be better company than you!" she shouted after him, but there was no answer. He had gone.

Now her anger began to cool. The cottage was so damp and dismal. She could hear odd creaks above her head that sounded like footsteps, though she knew there was nobody in the rooms upstairs. She had to keep reminding herself that she did not believe in ghosts. The only woman with a white face was likely to be herself, if Timon left her there too long.

Surely he wouldn't dare. Agnes and her mother would want to know what he'd done with her—unless they were all in it? No. That was stupid.

And yet people did kill for money. An old man was murdered the other day for the few pence he had in his pocket, it had been on the radio. How much did Dad's case hold? Thousands? Millions?

"You can scream if you like. No one will hear you," he had said. Did he mean to leave her here to die? Dead girls tell no tales. . . . She couldn't believe it. If only it wasn't so cold and dark and creepy in this wretched hovel.

She began to prowl around the house, testing the bars, kicking the front door, opening the cupboards. Timon was right: the bars were firm and the door solid. There was a damp, stained mattress on the floor of the other downstairs room, and in the kitchen cupboard she found a small iron frying pan, rusty and heavy. She carried it upstairs.

The window in the back bedroom broke easily beneath its weight, but it took her a long time to remove the jagged shards of glass that fringed the window frame. When at last she had finished, she leaned out of the window and looked down. The nettles here were not as thick as in the front, and she could see a large patch of uneven, stony ground beneath her, glittering with broken fragments of glass. Most of these lay flat but some stuck up from the earth like crystal teeth. It was not an encouraging sight. Also it seemed a long way down.

She had meant to hang by her hands from the sill and let herself drop, but she didn't feel like it anymore. There was a drainpipe on the wall. She leaned forward and stretched out her arm. Her fingers nearly touched it. Nearly but not quite. What now?

The sill jutted out on either side of the window. If she stood at the very end, she'd be able to reach the pipe without even letting go of the window frame with her other hand. Perfectly safe. What was she waiting for? Timon to come back?

She climbed out onto the sill. At first everything went well. The old wood did not crack. Her outstretched arms easily spanned the gap between the window and the pipe. If only her hand had been bigger or the pipe less fat —it was impossible to get a decent grip when her fingers only reached halfway around. Now she ought to let go of the window frame and move her left hand over. She didn't want to. It would be like throwing away an anchor when you found yourself on the edge of the world, with the sea falling over into space. But she could not stay here forever.

She began to wobble. Her right hand was slipping

down the pipe. She grabbed at it with her left hand, and now both hands were slipping down and down, painfully over the rough, flaking paint. Suddenly her fingers caught at something hard and clung.

She was suspended, like a lopsided hammock, her fingers clinging to one of the iron brackets that held the drainpipe to the wall, her toes hooked over the window-sill and higher than her head. Her eyes were tight shut, not wanting to see the mess she was in.

Timon, coming around the corner to see where she'd got to, stared up at her in horrified amazement.

"Hold on!" he shouted, running forward.

She opened her eyes, saw his upturned face below her; then her fingers gave way and she fell.

Chapter Fifteen

IT WAS a miracle, they told each other later, sitting over scrambled eggs on toast in the Welcome Café, a miracle they hadn't been killed. Elinor had landed on top of Timon, almost breaking his shoulder, or so he claimed, and knocking him backward onto the stony, glass-slivered ground, ripping a long slit in the sleeve of his denim jacket and a matching scratch on the skin beneath it.

"My jacket was new," he grumbled, though it obviously wasn't, being faded and worn and stained on one shoulder with green paint. "I only bought it last week from Oxfam."

There was no animosity in his voice. The collision had brought them closer together in more than the obvious way. They sat like old friends comparing battle scars, each boasting that their bruises were the bigger.

"I wish I could show you the ones on my bottom," Timon said, "but decency forbids it. They'd turn us out of here."

They laughed. They were happy to be still alive. The fear on Timon's face when he asked Elinor if she was all right—could she move her arms, her legs?—had turned to joy when she'd got shakily to her feet. It was obvious then that he'd never meant to hurt her. He had only wanted to scare her into giving him the key.

"How was I to know you'd do anything so stupid?" he asked. "There was no need to go throwing yourself out of windows. You can't really have thought I'd leave you there all night. I told you yesterday I'd promised Ma I'd look after you."

She did not tell him the terrible things she had thought.

They were sitting at a table by the window. The April sunlight streamed in through the glass, making them as warm as summer. The café was crowded with workmen from the building site having a late lunch, and one or two shoppers, whose feet hurt, having an early tea. The food was good and hot and cheap, unlike that in the Singing Kettle, but there was a lot of noise. They had to sit with their heads almost touching in order to hear themselves speak.

He told her he'd gone back to their bikes to get a bar of chocolate from his saddlebag. Having by then decided to admit failure and let her out, he thought he'd better have something to sweeten her temper, seeing that he'd eaten all the sandwiches. On the way back he'd heard the sound of banging and breaking glass, and had started to run.

"Running through holly isn't a good idea," he told her. "I must have left half my hair on those damn bushes, and look at my hands! When I reached the cottage, I couldn't see you anywhere. Then I went around the back and saw all the broken glass. I looked up—God! I was scared witless. There you were, hanging between the window and the drainpipe like a bit of old washing. You do realize that if you'd broken your neck, I'd have been blamed for it?"

"With good reason."

"Not at all. You were overreacting. Like I said, I only meant to scare you a little. To be honest, I didn't really expect it to work—you don't scare easy, do you?—but I felt I had to try. I couldn't just sit back and do nothing. Ma's been good to me. You don't know what she's like. You've never seen her at her best. She's changed a lot since we had to come and live with Aggie. She hates being dependent. She feels she's a nuisance and it makes her behave badly." He turned on Elinor in sudden anger. "How could your dad have done it to her, his own aunt! He might've left her something. Their house in Nettley didn't belong to them, you know—it went with Mr. Carter's job. They'd been saving up for somewhere to go when he retired, a garden apartment or a small cottage. . . . But your dad came along, all smiles and promises, and cheated her out of every penny, after her old man had died."

Her face flushed and she shouted furiously, "He didn't! I won't believe it!"

"Ssh! The waitress is coming."

She was a middle-aged woman in blue overalls, with small, bright eyes that looked at Elinor curiously, and a nose that twitched as if scenting a scene, a little entertainment in a boring day, something to talk about when she got home that night.

"Two doughnuts, please," Timon said quickly, while Elinor looked down at the table, forcing back her tears.

"Two doughnuts. Everything all right, dear?" the woman asked.

"Yes. Thanks," Elinor said, without looking up. The waitress lingered by their table, brushing away a few crumbs and altering the position of the sauce bottles. Then, as they remained silent, she shrugged, said once more, "Two doughnuts," and went away.

As soon as she'd gone, Elinor whispered fiercely, "I don't know why you're so darn self-righteous. It's not as if you're the soul of honesty yourself, is it?"

"How do you mean?"

"You told me you'd promised Ma you'd never steal again. *Again,*" she stressed the word pointedly.

"I knew it," he said. "I knew from the look in your eyes that you'd noticed. I could practically see you chalking the word up in the back of your mind, to use against me later. All right. So I was a thief once. That's how I met Ma, by the way. She caught me one night—"

"You mean you were stealing from her? Like Dad?"

"It was different," he said furiously. "Quite different. I didn't know her. She wasn't *my* aunt. She was nothing to me then. It was like stealing apples from a tree. Besides, I was only seven, not a grown man like your dad. I didn't have a big house in London and a posh car and money in the bank. I was just a skinny miserable kid in a children's home—The Gables, God, what a dump! I'd have run off again if—"

He broke off as the waitress came back.

"Two doughnuts," she said, putting the plates down on the table and walking away.

"Funny. There were doughnuts for tea the first day I was there," Timon said, looking at them. "I think they'd forgotten I was coming because there wasn't one for me. A big boy gave me his. 'Catch, kid,' he said, and threw it over. My hands were all covered with sugar and there was jam running down my chin. I must've looked like a regular idiot, sitting there and staring at him like he was God or something."

"He sounds nice," Elinor said.

"He was. They were all nice to me, his gang. I found out why later. They wanted me because I was small enough to get through those tiny windows people think it's safe to leave open. I was so thin in those days, you could practically post me through a mail slot. They used to toss me up onto a flat roof and I'd wriggle through a bathroom window and creep down to let them in."

"Not so nice, after all," Elinor said. "They were just making use of you."

Timon shrugged. "I bet they soon regretted it. I didn't bring them luck. The first time, I knocked over a small table and we all had to run for it. I broke their flashlight. Then a dog nearly got me. The last time Ma did." He smiled, his face softening with affection. "She was great."

"What did she do?"

"She gave me some milk and a big piece of fruitcake. Then she told me it was either her or the police, I could take my choice, but if I chose her, I must promise on my honor never to steal again. I chose her. I had to go back to The Gables for a bit, of course, while she fixed it up officially for me to stay with her. She didn't let them know —about finding me in her house, I mean. She never let on."

"What about the gang? Didn't they force you to go out with them again?"

"No. I think they were glad to be rid of me. They were worried at first in case I told their names, but I promised I wouldn't. And I won't, not to anyone. He was kind to me, the one who threw the doughnut."

What a childhood he must have had, Elinor thought, that a doughnut and a slice of cake could earn his gratitude and loyalty forever.

"Would you like mine?" she asked, pushing her plate toward him. "I haven't touched it. I could do with a friend like you."

He smiled but shook his head. "I'm on Ma's side. I can't be your friend while you're against her."

"I'm not, not anymore."

He leaned toward her, his eyes bright and hopeful. "Then give her back her money. Why don't you? Only what your dad took from her. I don't care about the rest. You can keep it. Please, Elinor, give her back her money."

She wanted to put her hands over her ears to shut out his soft, persuasive voice. His loyalties were different from hers. "I don't know," she said, "I don't know what to do."

"You don't have to trust me with it, if that's what's bothering you. Give it to her yourself. That would be best. You could pretend your dad asked you to. You could say he hadn't put it into his company after all— he'd had second thoughts. It might even be true."

Could it be? Elinor wondered. But he'd wanted Sophia to have it. . . .

"I don't know," she said again. "I can't think. My head aches. Give me time, give me till the end of the month."

"Till the end of the month, then," he said.

Chapter Sixteen

THAT NIGHT Elinor dreamed she was kneeling in a large, empty hall. The suitcase was on the floor in front of her. She touched the locks with an iron key and immediately the lid sprang open and money poured out, a flood of banknotes, some floating loose, some done up in bundles and fastened with rubber bands.

Suddenly a crowd of people surrounded her, jostling and elbowing their way forward. "That's mine!" an old woman said, and other voices joined in. "No, mine! It's mine! Mine!" They all began helping themselves, stuffing banknotes into their pockets and down their blouses and into their mouths.

"Don't eat it! It hasn't been cooked properly. You'll get salmonella," Elinor shouted, and everybody vanished. There was only the empty case and herself, sitting on the cold pavement beside the high prison wall.

"Elinor! Elinor!" her father's voice called reproachfully, and she woke up.

A stupid dream, she thought, shivering. Her quilt was on the floor. She pulled it back onto the bed and curled up beneath it, hugging her knees, trying to get warm again. Outside the window the sky was pale. Soon it would be time to get up and go to a new school, where everyone knew about her father. She didn't want to think about that.

She didn't want to think about the stolen money either. All yesterday evening her mind had been swinging backward and forward—should she, shouldn't she, hand it over to Mrs. Carter?

She had looked across the supper table, searching the fierce old face for any sign of the kindness Timon had described, and finding none. Hunched in her black shawl, the old lady had looked like a vulture waiting for somebody to die. Listen to her complaining to poor Aggie that the chicken wasn't cooked enough. She wouldn't have fed a young burglar on milk and cake, she'd have roasted him.

Yet Timon hadn't been lying then, Elinor thought, remembering the look on his face. It really happened. I'd stake my life on it. . . .

Her life but not the money.

She lay in bed, trying to think of a new hiding place, one that Timon would never guess. It was difficult. The house was so small and there were no hollow trees in the garden, no loose floorboards in the attic. Where on earth could she put it?

Next morning Elinor cycled to school by herself. Two boys had called for Timon and they had gone off noisily together, without his saying good-bye.

"They always go together, those three," Agnes said, looking anxiously at Elinor to see if she minded being left out. "You'll be all right by yourself, won't you, dear? Timon said he'd shown you the way."

"Yes. I'll be fine."

"It's always difficult, the first day at a new school, isn't it? I tell you what, I'll buy a cream cake for tea so you'll have something to look forward to. Though I'm sure you'll like it there, once you've settled down. Everyone says what a good school it is and—"

"Stop fussing, Agnes," Mrs. Carter said. She had got up for breakfast, instead of staying in bed as she usually did, and seemed unusually cheerful. "You'll only make the child nervous. Quite unnecessary. Timon says she'll do, and I gather that's high praise."

She smiled at Elinor who, surprised, smiled back, forgetting that she disliked the old lady. Perhaps Timon was right. Perhaps she wasn't so bad after all, once you got used to her. But poor Agnes, always so anxious and so polite, never seemed to have got used to her.

Timon was waiting for her outside the school gates. "Thought I'd better show you where to put your bike," he said, "seeing that it's Aggie's. We don't want it to get lost."

He took her along a concrete path around the side of the school, to a long bicycle shed, already nearly full, and stood watching while she padlocked it to a metal stand.

"Not that anyone would want to steal it," he said, "an old wreck like that."

"It goes all right."

"Something else went all right, didn't it? In the middle of the night. Where have you put it?"

"Put what?" she asked, trying unsuccessfully to look as if she didn't know what he was talking about. His face was hard and angry. He no longer looked as if he thought she'd do. He looked as if he wanted to shake her.

"The case," he said.

"What makes you think I moved it?"

"I looked. I sneaked up to the attic while you were having breakfast. What did you think I was doing? Taking a bath?"

"I didn't know," she said, smiling, but he didn't smile back.

"You never meant to give Ma her money back, did you? You didn't want time to think about it, you wanted time to hide it somewhere else. You were afraid I'd clip it. Once a thief, always a thief, that's what you thought, didn't you?"

"No! It wasn't that!"

"Why did you move it, then?"

She couldn't think of a convincing lie. She had, of course, been afraid that he wouldn't be able to resist all those thousands, perhaps millions, of pounds, but she didn't want him to know this. She didn't want him to be her enemy. Fortunately some boys came to put their bicycles nearby, and this gave her time to think. When the boys had gone, she said, "I only moved it because the water tank was making such odd noises. I was afraid Agnes would get a plumber in, and he'd find it—"

"Save your breath. I'm not stupid," he said, interrupting her. "You needn't have worried. I wouldn't touch your dirty money. It stinks. I wonder you can bear to sleep next to it. Didn't the thought of them keep you awake at night, all those poor old people like Ma, who lost all their savings? Didn't you fancy you could hear them, groaning and moaning all night long—"

"That was the water tank," Elinor said, refusing to cry.

He snorted, turned abruptly, and walked away. Elinor followed him slowly, feeling angry and shaken. It nearly made her late. A girl was waiting for her by the entrance.

"Are you Elinor what's-your-name?" she asked.

"Forest. Yes."

"The deputy head wanted to see you but you've missed her now. She had to go. You're to come with me to assembly. I'll show you where to leave your things first. Hurry up."

The girl's name was Janet Richards. She was fair and plump, and looked sulky, as if she wasn't at all pleased to have been told to take care of Elinor.

"You look old enough to be allowed out on your own," she said. "I don't know why I've got to be your nursemaid. Nobody looked after me when I came here. I had to find my own feet like anybody else. I suppose they think that because you've been to a private school, you must be soft."

"I'm not," Elinor said mildly, hanging her coat up in the locker Janet showed her. She didn't want to quarrel on her first day. She had enough to worry about without that. "How did you know I'd been to a private school?" she asked.

Janet shrugged. "Somebody told me."

"I suppose that same somebody told you my dad's in prison?" Elinor said, thinking she might as well have it out in the open now. Get it all over with at once. It looked like this was going to be a bad day.

The girl wriggled her shoulders. "Yeah, but that's nothing. I mean, I don't care if your dad's in the clink. It doesn't make any difference to me. My dad's no saint.

He's always swiping my pencils, and him a policeman and all."

"A policeman?"

"Yeah, a policeman," Janet said aggressively. "Want to make something of it?"

Elinor stared at her in surprise. "No. Why should I?"

The girl did not answer. The locker room was empty now. In the distance Elinor could hear voices, footsteps in the corridors getting fainter. She didn't want to be late for assembly on her first day.

"You think you are the only one with troubles," Janet muttered, going over to the mirror and beginning to comb her long, fair hair. "You should hear what some people call my dad. Funny, isn't it? Some are sniffy about your dad because he's in prison and some are sniffy about mine because he locks people up. Perhaps that's why they chose me to show you around. They thought we'd have something in common—having unpopular dads. You could almost say they were in the same line of business, only on different sides, like farmers and foxes. Or—" A bell rang in the distance and she said quickly, "Hell, we'll have to move. Come on. We can run, which is against the rules, or we can be late for assembly, which is also against the rules. You choose."

"Let's run," Elinor said.

They raced down the corridor together, catching up with other hurrying latecomers, and arrived just in time, breathless and smiling. It's not going to be such a bad day after all, Elinor thought. I'm going to survive. I like this girl, we might even become friends, who knows? That would be a joke, the daughters of a thief and a policeman. . . .

Chapter Seventeen

I<small>T WAS</small> warm and sunny for the rest of the week. Leaves and flowers burst out everywhere, even in the neglected garden of Number 7, Canal Walk. Coming home from school on Thursday, Elinor found Mrs. Carter crouching on the path. She ran forward, thinking the old lady had fallen. Then she noticed she was holding a trowel and kneeling on a rubber mat.

"Ought you to be doing that?" she asked. "I mean, with your bad leg?"

"Don't bully me," the old lady grumbled. "My leg's better now."

"But won't it make it bad again?"

"Probably. Why do you have to be so sensible? It's such a lovely day. I was beginning to feel young again. You never saw my garden in Nettley. There wasn't one to match it. . . . Of course, poor Aggie hasn't got the time. Still, you're perfectly right, I shouldn't be doing this."

"I'll do it for you," Elinor offered. "I'd like to."

"Can you tell a weed from a plant?"

"Not for certain," Elinor admitted. "Not unless they're

in flower. When they're small, they both have green leaves, it's confusing."

"And naturally you always had a gardener at home," Mrs. Carter said, but with a smile to show she was teasing. The fine weather suited her. She'd become quite human. Nothing could make her look like a sweet old lady, her face was too strong and irregular, but the smile improved it immensely.

"You've come at the right time," she went on, moving her legs and wincing. "I was just beginning to wonder if I was going to be able to get up again. How strong are you? Do you think you can help me?"

It wasn't easy. The old woman, though thin, was heavy and her legs had stiffened. Back on her feet, she staggered and grasped Elinor's shoulder to recover her balance. "Thank you," she said, and without letting go, turned to look at the girl's face for a moment. "You take after your father, don't you? In appearance, I mean. Same dark eyes and those lashes. . . . But you don't smile as much. I suppose that's only natural in the circumstances."

"What was Dad like when he was young?" Elinor asked.

"Spoiled," Mrs. Carter said, and plucking her stick out of a bush where she'd left it, went limping back into the house. Elinor followed her, bringing in the mat and the trowel. Once in the living room, the old lady lowered herself carefully onto the sofa, waving Elinor away when she tried to help.

"I can manage. I can manage. There's no need to hang over me," she said testily. "I'm sure you have better things to do."

"Not at the moment," Elinor said. "Tell me about Dad. I feel I don't know him, I don't understand him anymore."

"I shouldn't imagine you ever did. I certainly didn't understand my parents, any more than they understood me. I don't know what I can tell you. I'm not the right person to ask. I'm prejudiced. I'd only be rude about him and you'd get angry."

"Didn't you ever like him, not even when he was a child?"

"Yes. Yes, I did. He was rather a nice boy, I seem to remember. Very good looking. Spoiled, of course, but no more than many boys. Lily—your grandmother, I don't suppose you remember her, do you? You were only a baby when she died. Lily made too much fuss of him, for my taste. We had to stop talking when he came into the room in order to admire him. Poor Lily, she thought the world of him. She always said he'd do great things one day. I'm glad she can't see him now."

Mrs. Carter sighed and was silent, listening to old echoes out of the past, hearing again the children's voices as they played on the lawn; the dark, laughing boy and poor little mousy Agnes, following him everywhere, adoring him, grateful for a careless smile, a kind word. And he had been a kind boy, she remembered.

"I don't know what went wrong," she said, half to herself. "He had a happy childhood. Loving parents. No worries, not even about passing his exams, though he wasn't particularly clever. Lily was the one who worried. He'd just laugh and tell her not to fuss. 'I'll get through all right,' he said, and he always did. He never believed things could go wrong for him. He used to say he was lucky." She sighed. "Perhaps that was the trouble. He began to rely on luck. It made him a gambler. You know, I always found it hard to believe he deliberately set out to—" Catching sight of Elinor's face, she broke off abruptly.

"To cheat you out of your money," Elinor finished for her.

"Who told you? Agnes?"

"No. You made it pretty obvious," Elinor said, not wanting to give Timon away.

"I'm sorry," Mrs. Carter said stiffly. "I behaved very badly to you when you first came. I had no excuse."

"It doesn't matter."

There was a pause. Then Mrs. Carter said, "How is he?"

"I don't know. He won't let us visit him. He refuses to see anyone except Sophia and Mr. Brimly. And now Sophia's gone back to Italy."

"What made her go? Did she say?"

"Bambi had a cold. And it was snowing."

"What nonsense! Is that really the excuse she gave? Of course, she's very young, far too young. . . . Who's this Mr. Brimly?"

"The lawyer."

"Is he any good?"

"I don't know. Dad asked for him, so he must think so. And Sophia said he was very kind."

"Did she? Hmph. Why hasn't he got your father out on bail? I thought he was going to appeal against the magistrates' decision?"

"Dad doesn't want bail."

"Why ever not?"

Elinor shrugged. "Sophia said it must be because he was ashamed to show his face, but Janet—she's my new friend at school—she thinks it means he's going to plead guilty. He'll probably get a shorter sentence that way. Her father's a policeman so she knows about that sort of thing. It'd be the sensible thing to do, she said."

Mrs. Carter raised her eyebrows. "So you think he's guilty?" she asked.

Elinor did not answer.

"Well, well," the old lady said. "Poor George, why this lack of faith from his nearest and dearest? Mind you, you're probably right, but it still surprises me. I'd have expected you to swear blind that he was innocent. I must say, I hope if I'm ever accused of lifting a box of corn-flakes from our local supermarket, Agnes will be more ready to give me the benefit of the doubt."

Elinor flushed. She had been loyal to Dad. She'd never told anyone except Matthew about the luggage receipt, never admitted even to herself how angry she felt with him, how betrayed by what he'd done. She was tempted to fetch the case from its new hiding place and throw it down in front of the old lady, saying, "What do you think is in here? Pajamas?" It would be almost worth it to see her face when the stolen money spilled out over the worn carpet. Would she fall upon it wolfishly like the old woman in her dream?

She'd been happy when she came back from school. The sun had shone all day and she'd had no battles to fight. People had gone out of their way to be friendly. A girl called Sue had asked her to her birthday party on Saturday, and tomorrow she was going to tea with Janet. She wished she'd never asked Mrs. Carter about Dad. She didn't want to have to feel sorry for him all the time.

"What am I supposed to think?" she cried furiously, close to tears. "All he's ever said is that he's sorry. That's what he told Sophia to tell us—he's *sorry!*"

She would have run from the room, but Mrs. Carter caught hold of her hand, saying contritely, "I'm a stupid old fool. I keep forgetting how young you are. You're usually so calm and self-assured. . . . I didn't mean to upset you. Come here." She pulled Elinor down onto the sofa beside her and began patting her on the back, in a rather unpracticed sort of way, more like someone trying to bring up a baby's wind than offering comfort. "There, there. Poor girl, you've had a horrible time, and all by yourself too. But you're not alone now. We must see what we can do to help. I'll have a word with Agnes about it. Here, take my hanky. It's quite clean. And try not to feel too badly about your father. I expect those partners of his fooled him. George was never a mean boy. He wouldn't have wanted people to suffer. He just took one gamble too many. I'm sure it never occurred to him that things could go wrong."

Then it should have, Elinor thought bitterly. He hadn't needed to steal. He'd had a house, a big car, and money in the bank. As Timon had pointed out, Dad hadn't been a poor skinny little kid in a housing project. Why had he done it? Was he greedy? She didn't know. She'd always taken him for granted, loved him without question. You don't ask yourself if people deserve to be loved, do you? And yet she felt cheated.

Mrs. Carter was still patting Elinor on the shoulder when Timon came into the room.

"Oh, hello," he said, staring and backing out hastily. "I was just looking for Aggie. Isn't she home yet? I'm starving. I'll go and put the kettle on."

Later, when Elinor joined him in the kitchen, he asked eagerly, "Were you telling her about the money?"

"No!"

"Oh. I thought perhaps you'd told her and she was thanking you. I mean, it sort of looked like an emotional scene to me."

"We were talking about Dad."

"Oh." He opened a box of cookies and offered her one. "You didn't look as though you were quarreling," he said, sounding puzzled. "Usually when Ma talks about your dad, she gets very heated. Are you sure that you didn't just hint that she might get her money back?"

"No, I didn't! Don't badger me. It's not the end of the month yet. I've still got five days. I'll tell you on Wednesday, as I promised."

"I don't know how I can wait," he said, smiling at her. "But I'll have to, won't I? Seeing I don't know where you put the case."

He picked up the tray and went whistling out of the kitchen, leaving her looking after him uneasily. She recognized the song he was whistling. They were always playing it on the radio—

> "My baby's in hot water,
> Hot water, hot water.
> He did what he didn't oughta,
> The bad, bad boy."

It might, of course, be only a coincidence that she had hidden the case behind the boiler in the airing cupboard outside his room, but somehow she didn't think so. She had better move it again.

Chapter Eighteen

On SATURDAY morning a letter came for Elinor from her father. She looked down at the envelope Agnes handed her and recognized the writing, big and bold and unchanged. For some reason this annoyed her. She'd been worried sick about him. He'd always been at the back of her mind like a shadow; even when she was laughing with Janet at school, he'd been there. When she dreamed of him at night, he was usually pale and ill, shrunken and crinkled like an expiring balloon. And here was his handwriting, cheerful and confident as ever, with curly flourishes like party streamers.

The mail had come while they were at breakfast. Mrs. Carter must have recognized the writing too. When Elinor looked up they all looked quickly away, pretending they hadn't been watching her. She wondered if she'd turned pale and if they'd noticed that her hands were shaking. She put the letter on her lap and went on eating her scrambled eggs.

There was a silence while the others tried to think of something to say. Agnes remarked that it was raining, which they all knew, since the wind was blowing spatters of rain against the window and the clouds were so dark that they had to have the light on to see what they were eating. "Why does it always have to rain at weekends?" she asked.

Nobody answered. Timon grunted and picked up the paper. Elinor went on eating scrambled eggs. Mrs. Carter leaned forward and said, "Why don't you take your letter up to your room and read it in peace. You can take your plate with you. You'll only give yourself indigestion, bolting your food down like that. Go on."

Elinor thanked her and ran quickly upstairs. The letter was short; even his large writing could not cover more than one and a half pages.

My dearest Elinor,

Thank you for your letters. They have been a great comfort to me. I know you will forgive me for not having written before. You've always been such a kind girl, Ellie. You'll understand how difficult it's been for me.

I had a letter from Sophia today. She sends her love and asks me to tell you she'll be coming back to England shortly, so that you can all be together again.

I miss you all very much.

With lots and lots of love to you and Matthew and Judy,

Dad

She read it over and over again, then folded it slowly and put it in her pocket. The letter, though long in love, was remarkably short of information. Nothing about the date of the trial. Nothing to say he was going to plead guilty. No concealed hint about the luggage receipt or the money. He was treating her like a child, giving her sweets to keep her happy. It was Sophia he confided in, not her.

A knock at the door made her jump.

It was Timon, bringing a tray. "Here's some coffee. You'll see I've brought two cups," he said, putting the tray down on the chair. "One's for me—or would you rather I went away?"

"No."

"Aggie seems to regard a letter from your dad like a dose of flu—something you need time to recover from. She was going to make some of her revolting herbal tea and bring it up herself, but I said you'd rather have coffee and me. Was I right?"

"Yes."

He glanced at her face, then sat down on the bed beside her, putting his arm around her shoulders and placing a fairly clean handkerchief in her hands.

"I'm not going to cry," she said. "I never cry."

"You could have fooled me. The roof must be leaking."

She smiled and sniffed, and wiped her cheeks with his hanky. They sat for a moment in a comforting silence. Then, suddenly embarrassed, she moved away from him to take her coffee off the tray.

"I don't know why I am upset," she said. "It's not as if there's any bad news. In fact, there's very little news of any sort. You can read it, if you like," she said, taking it out of her pocket and handing it to him.

"I see you've always been a kind girl," he said, when

he'd finished. "That's news to me. I'm glad to hear it. And Sophia's coming back shortly. Is she your stepmother?"

"Yes."

"What's she like?"

"She's a bitch. No, she isn't. I'm just being jealous," Elinor said honestly. "I like her, actually. You can't help liking Sophia. She's so pretty and friendly. I bet all the men in Naples want to marry her. Poor Dad, I wonder if she really will come back."

"You can always stay with us if she doesn't," he told her.

She was surprised and touched. He'd sounded as if he wanted her to stay. But she couldn't, not for long. Even if Sophia didn't come back, she'd have to think of some way that she and Matthew and Judy could be together again. Judy was all right, but the last time she had phoned Worthing, Matthew had sounded cagy, answering briefly yes or no, as if enemies were listening.

He'd probably got on the wrong side of Mrs. Shaw, not a difficult thing to do, Elinor thought, remembering the thin, sharp woman, each of whose sides was as bad as the last; her scolding, her preaching, her sneers. . . .

Poor Matt, I should never have let him go to them, but he seemed to be getting on well with Mr. Shaw. And what could I do? I couldn't have shared a room with their two boys, not at my age. Perhaps it was just a bad day. Matt's always been moody. I'll call him up and tell him about Dad's letter, that will cheer him up.

Nobody answered the telephone when she rang later that morning, though she tried three times. It was Susie's birthday party in the afternoon and she did not get back till late. When she tried again on Sunday, Mr. Shaw answered. Matthew was out, he said. He'd gone down to the beach as soon as he'd finished breakfast. "He loves going for walks by himself, doesn't he?" Mr. Shaw said. "I was just the same when I was a boy. The sea fascinated me."

"Is he—" She'd been going to ask if Matthew was happy with them, but perhaps that would sound rude. "Does he like his new school?" she asked instead.

"I think so. He doesn't tell us much. He's a very quiet boy, isn't he? Not like our two. Of course, Pete and Ken are older than he is and they have their own friends— not that they mean to exclude him but you know what boys are. And he does seem to prefer his own company. Some children are naturally solitary, aren't they?" he asked, almost as if seeking reassurance. "And he must be missing you all, poor fellow."

"Can you ask him to call me when he comes in?" she asked.

To her surprise he said awkwardly, "Couldn't you write a letter or send a card? Only, my wife doesn't let our own boys use the telephone except in an emergency, otherwise they'd be chatting to their friends for hours. We have to think of the telephone bills, you know." Behind his embarrassed, hesitant voice she could hear another one, high pitched and scolding, saying, "Ask her if she thinks we're made of money."

"It's all right," she said quickly. "It doesn't matter. It wasn't anything urgent. Tell him I'll write." She hung up, wondering how much this call had cost and whether she ought to offer to pay Agnes for it. She'd never thought of doing so before.

The money Sophia had given her was dwindling rapidly, and yet she'd hardly bought anything much. Everything was so expensive. She was going to the cinema with Timon tonight and she could hardly expect Timon to pay for her. She frowned, trying to do sums in her head.

Before she fell asleep that night, she remembered she hadn't written to Matthew. I must do it tomorrow, she thought, I bet that awful woman is giving him hell. She never wanted him, she made that quite plain. It was Mr. Shaw who did. I bet they had a row about it before they came. I'm surprised he won. . . . Perhaps he said it was her duty. She was keen on people doing their duty, I remember. Poor Matthew.

No sooner had Mr. Shaw put down the telephone after Elinor's call, than his wife said sharply, "Don't tell that boy his sister called, will you?" She always spoke of Matthew like this. Pete and Ken were *her* boys, but Matthew was that boy, nothing to do with her, not worthy even of being given a name.

She's never forgiven me for insisting we ask him to stay with us, Mr. Shaw thought. Poor boy, I wish I hadn't. He isn't happy with us and who can blame him? Not me.

Aloud he said, "Why not, dear? It might cheer him up. He's very fond of his sister."

"She only upsets him. Remember last time she called? It unsettled him for days. Crying and carrying on and refusing to eat his meals. He's difficult enough as it is, without his sister stirring him up."

"I thought what a nice girl she was. It's only natural he should miss her. I'm sure she doesn't upset him deliberately."

"What do you know about young girls?" his wife asked scornfully. "She's a troublemaker, that one. Too used to having her own way. Don't you tell him she called or I'll have something to say about it. I'm not going through all that again, just when he's quieted down."

"Matthew's too quiet," Mr. Shaw said, but his wife called him a fool.

"That boy can't be too quiet for my liking," she said.

Chapter Nineteen

MATTHEW HATED Mrs. Shaw. He hated her two boys, Pete and Ken, but not as much. They were older than he was, two solid, red-cheeked, fair-haired boys, who teased him whenever they were alone, calling him Matt the jailbird's son or Matt the Brat, or simply Doormat, pretending to wipe their feet on him when he lay in the narrow camp bed in the corner of their room.

They accused him of stealing their pencils or their socks or whatever else they happened to have mislaid, and seemed genuinely surprised when he cried.

"Can't you take a joke?" they asked, and Ken, who was the younger and the less boisterous of the two, told him he wasn't the only kid who had a dad in prison. There was one in his class at school and he didn't whine and snivel about it.

"You ought to toughen up, kid," he said, quite kindly. But the next moment, when he couldn't find his penknife, he was shouting, "Hey, you, Doormat, what have you done with it? Turn out your pockets before I kick you inside out."

Matthew took to going up to bed early, so that he

could pretend to be asleep when they came up. He'd lie with his eyes shut, listening while their whispers and laughter died away to soft snores. In the daytime he kept out of their way. On schooldays this was easy as, being older, they were already at the junior high, several streets away from the primary he went to. After school and on weekends he spent hours walking on the windy, stony beach, the hood of his parka pulled around his face and his hands in his pockets. Sometimes Mr. Shaw came with him and they would walk side by side, not saying much but in sympathy with each other, like two outcasts exchanging shy smiles.

There were even times when Matthew was happy, times when the tide was far out and a watery sun shone down on the wet, wrinkled sands till they gleamed like gray silk. Then he'd run with his arms held out like wings and the wind behind him, faster and faster, his bare feet splashing through the shallow puddles the sea had left behind. He'd fill his pockets with shells and feathers and glistening pebbles, some with fine green weeds attached to them like mermaid's hair. He hid these treasures under his bed, but Pete and Ken sniffed them out and made him throw them away, complaining that they stank the room out worse than his feet.

The beach was his private kingdom. The wind and doubtful weather kept most people away. The local boys had better things to do than paddle in the cold sea. There were only a few stubborn children, their icy hands clutching shrimping nets, the dog walkers, and early one morning, seven riders galloping by, their horses' hooves splintering the shallow green sea into a dazzling white. Matthew looked after them for a long time, so long that he was late for breakfast and Mrs. Shaw shouted at him, telling him off not only for being late but for having gone out at all.

"Leaving the front door unlocked so that anyone could walk in and out. Not even making your bed or tidying your things—"

"He leaves his dirty socks under his bed," Pete said.

"You filthy little beast!" she cried, wrinkling her nose with disgust. "I suppose you're used to servants clearing up after you. Well, let me tell you—"

"I didn't know where to put them," he interrupted, scarlet with shame.

"It didn't occur to you to ask?" she demanded. "What were you going to do when you ran out of clean socks? Go on wearing the dirty ones, I suppose, till they rotted on your feet."

"Leave the boy alone," Mr. Shaw said, but his wife didn't listen to him.

After breakfast she dragged Matthew upstairs and stood over him while he fished out his dirty socks from under the camp bed. Then she marched him down to the kitchen and made him wash them himself in the sink, refusing to let him use the washing machine, as if she thought he'd contaminate it. She had found his black shoes, rimmed with the whitish stains of salt water from the time he'd forgotten to take them off before running out onto the sands.

"Disgusting," she said. "Dirty, dirty, dirty boy! In future you're not to go down onto the beach, do you hear? I won't have you ruining your clothes. I can't afford to buy you new ones."

"You don't have to! Sophia will, when she comes

back!" he shouted, and felt a sudden longing for his step-mother. He forgot her faults and only remembered how pretty she was, how she'd laughed and hugged them and bought them silly presents, and how she'd cried when he wouldn't kiss her good-bye. "She loves us! She knows how to look after us properly," he said, and stepped back quickly, thinking Mrs. Shaw was going to hit him, she looked so spiteful.

"She loves you, does she? That's why she left you, I suppose. Couldn't get rid of you soon enough, if you ask me. You don't really think she's coming back, do you?"

Matthew did not answer. He just stood looking at her, quite calmly. It embarrassed Mrs. Shaw. Perhaps she shouldn't have said what she did, but he needn't think she was going to apologize. She never apologized.

"All right," she said. "You can go now."

"Yes," he said, and actually smiled. She looked after him uneasily, puzzled by his strange behavior. She did not know that he had decided to run away and already she was losing her power over him, like a nightmare from which he had woken up.

Whenever he was alone in the house, Timon had been searching for the hidden case. Elinor had moved it again and he could not find it. The house was so small. There weren't many hiding places. He had done the attic rooms and the cupboard under the stairs. He had gone through the kitchen and the garden shed. He'd poked about in the flower beds, looking for signs of disturbed earth, and climbed the old apple tree to see if it was hidden in the leaves.

No luck anywhere.

Time was running out. Today was Monday and on Wednesday she had promised to tell him her decision. He had to find it before then. It was not that he wanted to steal the case. His life of crime had ended when he was seven. Eating Ma's cake, he'd gladly promised to give it up. To tell the truth, he'd never really enjoyed all that hanging about in the chilly nights, squeezing through painfully small windows, being snapped at by slavering dogs—and for what? Even if they'd struck it lucky, they'd have had to keep it dark, and what was the fun of that? Timon liked to show off a little. He wanted people, girls especially, to admire him. He dreamed of being recognized in the streets and supermarkets, of hearing people whisper, "Look, isn't that Timon Carter, the great—actor, barrister, surgeon, politician—" He hadn't decided yet which.

He wanted to find the suitcase so that he could tell Elinor he knew where it was, that was all. He could not bear to think she had beaten him.

What could she have done with it?

He hoped it wasn't anything crazy—such as lowering it into the canal on a string and tying the other end to a bush, so that she could retrieve it later. It was the sort of nutty thing she might do. He might have done it himself once. He thought of all the dirty water seeping into the case, soaking all Ma's savings into a mushy pulp. He couldn't bear the thought. He put on his parka and ran out into the rain and the wind. There was nobody in sight. Elinor was late, probably having tea with that plump friend of hers.

Timon crossed the road, climbed the low wall opposite and slid down the short, steep bank onto the towpath. Then he began walking slowly, looking down into the brown water for a telltale piece of string. He was so absorbed in this that he didn't notice the small boy crouching in some bushes by the wall, turning his wet, white, terrified face to stare out at him through the leaves.

Timon walked on as far as the bridge and sheltered under it, glad to be out of the wind. There was no string dangling into the canal anywhere. It'd been a silly idea. He picked up a thin stick and poked it into the water, stirring up a smelly filth of mud and debris. Wrinkling his nose, he threw the stick away, and began to walk back.

As he passed the clump of bushes, a strong gust of wind suddenly made them curtsy and caper like mad things. He turned his head and found himself looking straight into a pair of frightened dark eyes. Before Timon could say anything, a small boy burst out of the bushes, clambered over the wall, and ran blindly across the road. Timon followed, but his feet slipped on the weedy bank and he climbed the wall only just in time to see the boy racing down the path that led past the end house in the terrace and on into the woods.

He gave chase instinctively but lost him among the trees. There were too many hiding places and the wind in the branches made enough noise to mask the foot-steps of a hundred runaways. Timon shrugged and shiv-ered. It was not an evening to play games in the woods, he thought. Not an evening to hide in bushes by the ca-nal, either, getting soaked to the skin. What had the boy been doing there? A young thief, perhaps, keeping look-out for his gang?

Timon turned and walked down the path behind the

houses in Canal Walk, looking for signs of a break-in. There were lights in most of the kitchen windows now, though it was only five o'clock. It was already getting dark and people were making themselves tea, needing something warm to comfort themselves for the change in the weather. He could see Mrs. Pearce filling her kettle at the sink, and as he passed the Johnsons' house, their Doberman set up a furious barking, hurling its weight against the kitchen door so that it shook and strained at the lock.

There were no back doors left ajar, no broken glass, no small windows open near flat roofs and convenient drainpipes. Canal Walk looked safe and warm. But as he turned to go home, he still felt uneasy. The small, frightened boy reminded him of someone. He was haunted by a feeling that he'd known someone like him once, someone he cared about and wanted to protect, but he couldn't remember who it was.

Perhaps it had been a long time ago. Somebody at The Gables, perhaps, one of the gang he'd gone about with? But they'd all been older and bigger—there'd only been one small member of the gang, and that had been himself.

He smiled sheepishly. Had the boy reminded him of himself? No wonder he'd wanted to protect him. Poor kid, he thought, I wish I'd caught him. I could have taken him home to Ma.

Chapter Twenty

By SEVEN the rain had stopped, but the wind was blowing fiercely. When Janet opened the front door, a rush of leaves came in, twisting and turning over the pink carpet.

"What a night," she said. "They said there'd be bad gales tomorrow. They seem to be starting early. You'd better wait for Dad. It'll only take him a minute to run you back in the car."

"I'll be all right," Elinor told her.

Her bicycle, which she'd left propped up against the wall of the house, was now lying on a clump of crushed tulips.

"I'm sorry. Look what I've done."

"The wind did it, not you," Janet said. "Are you sure you're going to be all right? It's pretty wild." The wind caught their long hair and tossed it over their faces so that they could hardly see. An empty plastic flowerpot suddenly sailed past them and crashed into the fence. "You'd better wait for Dad. He won't be long. Stay to supper, like Mom said—"

"I can't. I promised Agnes I'd be back early. She's taken her mother to London today and I said I'd get Timon his supper. Besides, I haven't done my essay yet. And I want to wash my hair."

"Excuses, excuses, too many excuses," Janet grumbled. "You're not fooling me, you know. You're afraid of Dad, aren't you? I dunno why. *You* haven't done anything. He thinks you're a nice girl. He said so. 'I like your new friend'—those were his very words."

"Obviously he's a man with good taste," Elinor said lightly, but she would not be persuaded to stay.

It was true, she never felt at ease with Janet's father. Whenever she saw him, in or out of uniform, she thought of the stolen money. When he looked at her, she felt herself change color guiltily. When he smiled, she thought of a cat playing with a mouse. She was being unfair to him, she knew, but she couldn't help it.

She wheeled her bicycle out into the road.

"Take care, Ellie!" Janet shouted.

"I will. Good-bye!"

The wind was behind her, pushing her forward like a cold hand on her back. It was exhilarating to be speeding through the dusk, her jacket flapping like a sail, her hair blowing wild, and the bicycle wheels hissing on the wet roads. She wished the journey would go on forever, on and on with the sky darkening and the stars coming out, with spring turning into summer, and this year into next; until all her problems had been left behind.

When she turned into Canal Walk, the wind caught her sideways, taking her by surprise. She swerved violently across the narrow road, hit the curb, and tumbled into some wet laurel bushes, with the bicycle on top of her. Its spinning back wheel glittered in the lamplight like an expiring pinwheel.

Timon, who had been looking out for her, came running up.

"If a car had been coming, you'd have been killed," he said angrily, lifting the bicycle off her and propping it up against the laurel. "What did you think you were doing—" He broke off abruptly and stared. Her face, as she looked up at him, was pale and her dark eyes wide with shock. He knew now whom the boy had reminded him of.

"You startled me," she said, as he helped her to her feet. "I didn't see you there. The wind blew me across the road. The bike's not damaged, is it?"

"No. Keep still a minute." He smoothed her long dark hair and held it loosely at the back of her neck so that it framed her face like a hood. "You've got a young brother, haven't you?" he asked.

She had thought for a startled moment that he'd been going to kiss her. Now she became frightened. "Matthew? What's happened?"

"Nothing. Don't panic," he said quickly. "It's only . . . I saw a boy who reminded me of someone. Does your brother look like you?"

"Not really. His hair's lighter. And he's only nine."

"The boy I saw could've been nine. I didn't see his hair. It was raining then and he had the hood of his parka up. It was his eyes, mostly—they might have been yours. He was hiding in those bushes over there, watching these houses."

"In the rain? Did you ask him what he was doing there?"

"I didn't get a chance," Timon said. "He shot off like a rabbit. I ran after him but he had too good a start."

"Where did he go?"

"Into the woods."

"Oh." A gust of wind pushed at them and rattled the bicycle against the laurels. She shivered. "Matthew's in Worthing," she said. "It can't have been him. How could he get here?"

"That's all right, then."

They went into the house. In the living room the table was already laid for two: ham salad, and apple pie and cheddar cheese.

"Would you like me to heat you up some soup?" he asked, but she didn't seem to hear him, so he added, "Why don't you call him up and put your mind at rest?"

Her face brightened and she ran out to the telephone in the hall, only to come back later, looking more worried than ever. "There's no answer. They must all be out. I rang twice in case I'd dialed the wrong number, but there's nobody there. Do you think they're out looking for him?"

"They've probably gone to a movie," he suggested. "Come and have your supper."

"I don't want any supper."

"I wish I'd never told you about that boy. It could've been anyone. It could've been one of the boys from the new development—"

"It could've been Matthew," she said. "Some people say we look a bit alike, our eyes. . . . He wasn't happy with the Shaws, I could tell he wasn't. I should never have let him go there." She looked at Timon with frightened, guilty eyes. "I've always known he's the sort of boy who'd run away. I meant to write to him last week but I forgot. I should've looked after him better."

Outside the window the trees strained and staggered in the wind and they could hear the sound of something —a tin can, perhaps—clattering down the road.

"I'm going out to look for him," Elinor said.

Timon tried to argue with her, offering to go himself, but it was no good. She was determined. He'd never met a girl before as stubborn as Elinor. All that he could do in the end was to find a flashlight that worked and go with her. It was only just half past seven. They had three hours before Ma and Aggie came back, time enough to search the woods and either find the boy, or convince Elinor he was not, and never had been, there.

Matthew was lost. He'd run into the woods like a hunted fox, thinking only of getting away. On and on he'd gone, following a faint track that he could hardly see. When at last his breath and legs had given out, he went to earth beneath a holly tree and lay, panting and shaking, waiting for the boy who'd chased him to give up and go home. But it was noisy in the woods, with the wind screaming in the branches above his head, and everything creaking and rustling. He'd never be able to hear footsteps: the tall boy could be creeping up on him now.

So he stayed crouching in the wet, prickly leaves, until the great crack and snapping rush of a falling branch sent him leaping out of his hiding place in terror. Then the nightmare began. Nowhere in the roaring dark seemed safe. All around him trees shuddered and groaned as if in pain. The air was alive with whirling leaves; like swarms of wild bees they stung his face and threatened his eyes as he stumbled over the shifting ground.

He'd have welcomed the tall boy then. He'd have welcomed anyone, but he was alone in the tormented woods, alone and lost. The faint track he'd been following had disappeared. He blundered through the dark from one tree to another.

"Keep away from trees," Elinor had told him after the great gales had swept through London, knocking over the flowering cherries in the suburbs and uprooting the silver birches in Highgate woods. "You don't want your head cracked open like a soft-boiled egg, do you? Think of the mess."

Keep away from trees—he wished he could, but they were everywhere, closing in, imprisoning him in a swaying, prickly basket of latticed branches. He shut his eyes and struggled to get out, forcing his way through with bleeding hands.

Suddenly he found himself in a clearing. The sky above his head was sprinkled with pale stars and a lopsided moon. In the middle of the clearing was a small house, like a child's drawing, with a front door in the middle, and a window shining faintly on the right-hand side. As he stumbled toward it, he saw that the bottom windows were barred and there was no light within. It had only been the moonlight that glimmered in the dusty glass. The front door was locked and nobody answered his frantic knocking.

The wind wailed behind him and he thought it was calling his name.

"Matthew! Matthew!"

He turned, and saw, coming out of some bushes, the dim figure of a woman with a white face.

Chapter Twenty-one

HE MIGHT have been a shadow, lying across the shallow doorstep, so still he was, and cold. Timon reached him first. Kneeling down, he took the small hand in his and fumbled for the pulse.

Elinor came rushing up and flung herself down beside them.

"Matthew! Matt!" she cried, taking her brother by the shoulder and shaking him. "Matthew! Wake up!"

"Careful! He could be hurt!"

"He's fainted. He's always fainting," she said, sounding both cross and frightened, as if she thought her brother did it on purpose to worry her. She put her cheek close to his mouth and felt with relief the faint warmth of his breath. "Did you think he was dead? We'd better get him out of this wind or he soon will be. Have you got the key?"

"Yes."

They carried him into the room on the right and laid him down gently on the damp, filthy mattress. It was warmer out of the wind, that was all you could say for it. Otherwise the stone cottage was as dark and dismal as any prison. Matthew's clothes were soaking wet and his face in the faint flashlight beam looked bloodless. They took their parkas off and tucked them around him, and loosened the strings of his hood so that he could breathe more easily. His eyelids flickered but remained shut. He was shivering.

"We need a fire," Elinor said. "He's so cold. He'll be ill if we leave him in his wet clothes." She shone the flashlight around the room. "There's all this old newspaper lying about, and plenty of wood outside."

"It'll be too wet," Timon said. "I suppose we could use the banisters to start it. . . . Have you any matches?"

"No. Haven't you?"

"No."

They looked at each other in dismay.

"I suppose he wouldn't have any?" Timon asked.

"I doubt it." She glanced down at her brother as she spoke and saw his eyes open a little and shut again quickly when she turned the flashlight toward him. "Matthew! Come on, I saw you. It's no good pretending you're still out. I know you're not."

"I expect he's frightened," Timon said. He knelt down beside the boy and said gently, "Don't worry about me. I'm on your side. You look as if you need friends. Nobody's going to be mad at you. I ran away once, so I know what it's like. It's lonely, isn't it?"

Matthew opened his eyes and stared at Timon, but did not say anything. A sudden crash outside made them all jump. Timon ran to the window and looked out.

"What is it?" Elinor asked.

"A tree. A tree's gone over."

"Is she still there?" Matthew asked, looking fearfully toward the window.

"Who?"

"The woman. Is she still there?"

"What are you talking about?" his sister asked. "What woman?"

"Out there. I heard her calling me. Then she came out of the woods—" His eyes were enormous with dread.

"That was me," Elinor said. "Only me. Did you think I was a ghost?"

Timon turned from the window. "You didn't tell him about the—"

"Shut up!" she said fiercely.

Matthew looked bewildered. "Tell me about what?" he asked.

"Nothing."

The wind shrieked in the chimney. Outside dark branches whipped across the white-faced moon.

"Was it really you?" Matthew whispered, turning to stare into his sister's face. "I can't see you properly. Can't we have the light on?"

"There isn't any light."

"I thought you were a ghost. You looked so funny."

"There aren't any ghosts, Matt," she said, putting her arm around him and frowning at Timon over his head. She didn't want to talk about white-faced women now.

"There are. I've seen them," Matthew insisted.

"No, there aren't." She rested her cheek against his damp hair and wondered what it was like to live inside his head, in a world still inhabited by ghosts and monsters, by creatures far stranger than a dream. At least, she thought ruefully, his dangers have their remedies:

cross fingers, touch wood, throw salt over your left shoulder, wear garlic in your buttonhole, and you will be safe. I wish my troubles could be warded off so easily.

"I don't think it's a good idea to go out yet," Timon said. "There's branches coming down all over the place. I saw one flying through the air like a broomstick just now. We'd better wait till the wind's died down. You don't have any matches, do you, kid?"

"In my bag," Matthew said.

They had forgotten his bag. It had been on the ground beside him, and they had brought it in. He had come well equipped for his journey. Matches, string, apples, half a loaf of brown bread, cheese, six lumps of sugar, a penknife, a small compass—and his schoolbooks. He had taken his books because this was his school bag and they belonged in there. He hadn't dared to leave them behind.

He had not thought of bringing a flashlight, though. They only had one and that was nearly out. When Timon went out into the hall to kick out some banister struts for their fire, he took it with them, leaving them in the dark, except for the pale, fretted moonlight that shifted across the floor beneath the window.

"Never mind, we'll have firelight soon," Elinor said. She had gathered up the old newspapers and was now folding and twisting them, as Timon had showed her, to make them burn longer. "What happened, Matt?" she asked. "Why did you run away?"

He didn't answer. A loud crack from the hall made him jump and catch his breath.

"It's only Timon breaking the banisters," Elinor told

him. "Don't worry, Matt. Don't worry about anything. You're all right now."

She could feel him shivering beside her and saw him peer at her through the darkness, as if still uncertain whether she wasn't a ghost.

"It was clever of you to find your way here all by yourself," she said.

"I got a train," he said, his face brightening up with pride. "I asked for a return ticket. People think you're coming back then. They don't think you're running away."

"That was clever," she said again. "Lucky you had enough money."

She knew at once, by the way he stiffened beside her, that she had said the wrong thing. She was afraid that he'd shut her out, as he sometimes used to shut everyone out when he was younger, lying on his bed with his face in the pillow, refusing to answer. But after a minute he began to speak, the words rushing out as if he was glad to be rid of them.

"I stole it. I had some money, but not enough. . . . She keeps some in a blue jug in the kitchen. I've seen her go there when the milkman comes for his money. Pete took some last week. He didn't know I'd seen him but I did. I saw him through the window. I knew I'd get blamed for it so I thought I might as well take the rest. That's why I can't go back. I can never go back. I'd rather die. I stole the money—"

"Borrowed," Timon said firmly, coming into the room with the broken wood in his arms. "You want to be careful with words, kid. Words are powerful. Never say you stole anything. You borrowed it, see?" He dropped the wood on the floor and knelt down by the grate. "You'd have asked her but she wasn't there and you couldn't wait. You're going to pay it back—how much was it, by the way?"

"Eighteen pounds and fifty pence."

"Right. Your sister will give it to you when we get home. She's got plenty of money," he said, with a sly look at Elinor. "Where are the matches? Thanks."

He had arranged the paper and wood while he was speaking, and now struck a match and held it to the edge of the paper. After a moment tiny flames ran up and flickered wildly in the draft from the chimney.

"We can send her a postal order," Elinor said.

"Yeah, with a nice polite letter thanking her for having him."

"It won't do any good. She hates me!" Matthew burst out. "She'll tell the police!"

"Let her," Timon said. "You can tell them a thing or two as well, can't you? Tell them she hates you. Tell them she frightened you and starved you and shut you up in the henhouse for hours. They'll believe you. Things like that happen. A boy I knew said his mom always put him in the chicken run when she went out, if it wasn't raining. This was when he was tiny, mind. I expect she thought it was as good as a playpen. Keep him safe. Trouble was he didn't like chickens. Those beady black eyes and sharp beaks and the sudden way they turn their heads. They gave him nightmares. He never got over it. Can't eat chicken to this day. The very sight of them makes him shake."

Matthew stared at him. "It wasn't anything like that," he said.

"Doesn't she keep chickens? Well, the broom closet would do. Better still, the cellar if she's got one. It doesn't have to be exactly true," Timon explained kindly. "Just give them the general gist. I mean, you can exaggerate a little, can't you? I always did. Cry, if you can. Whimper like the wind in the chimney. It works wonders, I promise you. You're lucky you're small. You'll have them all on your side."

"You don't know her," Matthew said. "She'd tell them I'm a liar! She'd tell them about Dad and say we were all thieves, and it's *true*! I won't see her again! I won't!"

Elinor put her arms around him and held him tightly, saying, "It's all right, Matt. You don't have to. We'll go away together, you and me and Judy. We'll find somewhere to live. I'll think of something. Don't worry."

"We've got all that money," he whispered.

She looked quickly at Timon and saw that he had heard. His face in the firelight looked resigned, as if he'd never really believed that she'd hand it over to Ma.

"I'm sorry," she said.

"What are you going to do?"

"I don't know. I'll think of something," Ellie said. The fire shifted in the grate, sending up a bright haze of sparks. She went over to it and, kneeling down, began to place more of the broken wood on top.

"You'll get yourselves murdered," Timon said, looking worried. "You don't know your way around. You don't know how nasty people can be. It's not easy when you're a kid. They'd kill you both for what's inside that case. Why don't you stay here? We could make it cozy. Buy things, sleeping bags, frying pans and food. Nobody ever comes here. Even if they did, they couldn't get in if you kept the door locked. I'll stay with you, if you like. We'd be safe here."

A sudden gust of wind roared through the trees outside and rattled the window in its frame. The fire flickered wildly and smoke came gushing out of the chimney. There was a tearing crash as the great tree fell onto the cottage, smashing through the roof and bringing down the ceiling of the room they were in.

Chapter Twenty-two

MATTHEW WAS choking. There was dust in his mouth, dust in his eyes, and his shoulder hurt. All around him there were noises; the sound of cars rushing past, wolves howling, and a sort of soft pattering, like hailstones on earth. He was lying down somewhere, but he couldn't think where. He couldn't remember. . . . It was so dark: he might have been blind.

Near him, someone called hoarsely, anxiously, "Elinor? Elinor?"

He sat up, pushing aside something stiff and awkward that had been resting on his shoulder. A cloud of dust rose up and set him coughing again so that he could not speak.

"Elinor? Is that you?" the voice asked hopefully, and a light flowered in the dark. He saw a boy coming out of a sea of broken plaster, holding a match in his hand. His face, his hair, even his eyelashes, were white with dust. Only his eyes were dark and fearful.

"Oh, it's you," the boy said, sounding disappointed. "Where's Elinor? Where's your sister?"

Matthew's head cleared. He knew now that the boy

153

was Elinor's friend, Timon. They were in a cottage in the middle of some woods and the ceiling had come down on their heads. There were no cars or wolves, only the wind in the trees outside.

"She was right beside you," Timon said, sounding accusing as if he thought it was Matthew's fault that they had lost Elinor. Matthew looked around. Dust hung like a white mist in the air, through which he could see dim shapes rising up from the rubble like pale icebergs.

"Ellie!" he cried wildly.

The match went out.

"Wait! Don't move!" Timon commanded urgently. "We don't want to bring the whole thing down on our heads."

Another match flared. They both looked around, narrowing their eyes against the dust and smoke—*smoke!*

"The fire!" Matthew cried, remembering. "She'd got up to put some more wood on the fire—where is it?" His voice rose hysterically. "Where's the fireplace gone?"

"It's behind there. Where the smoke's coming from. No! Don't rush at it!"

The match went out.

Matthew felt Timon's hand tight on his arm, restraining him. His voice came out of the darkness, saying that they'd got to keep their heads, half the ceiling was down, the other half would follow if they weren't careful. "I'll lift the loose plasterboard aside," he said. "I'm stronger than you. Look up there."

He struck another match. Looking up, Matthew could see an enormous gaping black hole, its jagged edges fringed with splintered laths and broken boards. Something huge and dark had elbowed through it, and half the ceiling was hanging down, resting precariously on a sharp corner that touched the floor.

"We don't want that on our heads," Timon said. "Take the matches—don't lose them, for God's sake. Can you light them one after another and hold them steady for me?"

"Yes."

But he could not hold them steady. His hand shook so much that the flames danced and dimmed. He had to tilt the matches down to keep them alight and they burned up more quickly that way. The darkness swallowed up the tiny circles of light like a toad snapping up fireflies. He had a series of brief glimpses of Timon lifting aside the loose pieces of broken plasterboard, the dust rising round his legs like the surf of a shallow sea. Then Timon was kneeling, peering under the lower edge of the hanging ceiling.

"She's here," he said, crawling forward.

Matthew moved too quickly; the match burned his fingers and went out. He fumbled with the box, nearly dropping it out of his shaking hands.

"She's alive," Timon said. "She's breathing oddly. I expect it's the dust. . . . Elinor? Ellie, can you hear me?"

There was no answer. Matthew at last managed to strike another match. He held it up but he could not see Elinor. Timon was in the way.

"Ellie?" he cried.

"She's unconscious," Timon said. "Her head's hurt. I'll have to move her. We can't leave her here. It may all come down at any moment and I don't like this smoke. . . . You'd think the fire would've gone out—perhaps it has. I don't know. I just don't know." He was silent, then he said, "I can't feel any broken bones or blood, I'll have to risk it."

He looked around. His face in the matchlight looked desperately worried and his eyes asked the questions he didn't put into words—Am I doing the right thing? Supposing she's badly hurt and I make her worse?

"I'll help," Matthew said. "Let me help."

"I'm going to drag her out by her shoulders. Can you keep the matches going so that I can see?"

He ducked his head and reached forward. His shoulder brushed an edge of the hanging ceiling and it swayed a little. The match in Matthew's fingers leapt and trembled wildly but kept burning. He saw Timon shuffling backward on his knees, holding Ellie half on his lap so that her head rested on his arm. Her eyes were shut and her mouth open. A dark stain of blood clung to her right temple like a black spider.

"Don't light another match yet," Timon said. "Let me get my breath first. Then I'll lift her up and carry her into the hall."

"I'll see if the way's clear," Matthew offered, longing to be doing something. The sound of his sister's harsh, difficult breathing frightened him. He could not bear to sit in the dark listening to it. He struck another match, gave his sister's pale, bloodstained face a quick, horrified glance, and then, getting to his feet, cleared a path through the debris to the door. The hall beyond was undamaged. He opened the front door and the wind came in, blowing the dust before it. He could see the moonlight now and the wild trees. It was cold. He shut the door and went back to guide Timon out of the wrecked room.

Timon laid Elinor gently down in the hall. She

moaned and turned her head restlessly, but her eyes remained shut and she didn't answer when they spoke to her.

"There're only five matches left," Matthew said.

"We can sit in the dark."

"But Ellie's hurt. We need a doctor. We need help. I'll go. I'm not afraid. I'll go and fetch a doctor."

"You don't know the way," Timon said. "I'm the one to go. I can run faster than you and I won't get lost."

"What are you waiting for, then?" Matthew asked resentfully. He was frightened of staying here with Elinor, frightened she'd die and there'd be nothing he could do. He'd rather run through the woods, risking falling trees and a cracked head, than feel forever that he might have saved Ellie if only he'd known what to do.

"It's the smoke," Timon said. "The smoke worries me. . . . She's heavy. I don't think you'd be strong enough to carry her outside if there was a fire. I could take her out now, I suppose, and leave you both in the shelter of a bush, but it's cold and the ground's wet. You might be dead when I got back, dead and covered with leaves, like the babes in the woods." He said this with a laugh, as if he was joking, but Matthew guessed it was a real fear. They were all cold and their jackets were buried somewhere beneath the rubble. They had nothing now but their shirts to wrap around Elinor.

"How are you feeling? Are you really better? Can you run?" Timon asked.

"Yes, I can," Matthew said eagerly, but was then suddenly doubtful. "If you tell me the way. Only, I got lost before."

"There's another way at the back of the house with a regular path. I'll show you."

"We can't leave her alone."

"No, no," Timon said reassuringly. "I'll carry her, a little way at a time. You run ahead and fetch help. The path comes out on the London road. You'll see some houses opposite. Tell them to call for an ambulance and bring a stretcher to meet me. Come on."

They went out into the wind and the uncertain moonlight, Timon carrying Elinor in his arms. Matthew looked up in fearful amazement at the great tree that rested its neck across the cottage, its branches, like a giant's unruly hair, hanging to the ground. They had to circle around them to get to the back of the house. Timon, stopping, said breathlessly, "There's the path. Over there."

"Look after her."

"Yes. I will. Don't get lost."

"I won't," Matthew said, and began to run.

"Take care!" Timon shouted after him. His voice, high above the sound of the wind, echoed through the woods until it seemed that every tree repeated the warning, "Take care! Take care!"

Glancing back through leaves, Matthew saw Timon sitting wearily on the wet ground, holding Elinor tightly in his arms. He turned his head and ran on doggedly down the path.

Chapter Twenty-three

ELINOR OPENED her eyes.

"Good, you've come to again," the old woman said. "You still look dazed. I suppose they gave you something to help you sleep. Aren't you going to say, 'Where am I?' Or do you remember?"

Elinor gazed around. A screen of flowered curtains surrounded her bed, shutting her in with the old woman. Above the curtains she could see the walls of a large room, the tops of six tall windows, and a high ceiling. The light was dim and gray and cool. It was very quiet. No sound of traffic. No sound of the wind. . . . She frowned, suddenly anxious, but not knowing why.

"Do you remember who I am?" the old lady asked.

Elinor looked back at her. She saw a fierce old face, a thin face with a nose as sharp as a beak, the face of an old crow. The dark, baggy eyes were surprisingly kind.

"You're Timon's Ma," she said, remembering. "Oh, are they—?" She tried to sit up but Mrs. Carter pushed her back onto the pillows, saying, "They're both all right. We told you when you came around last night but I expect you've forgotten. You were very confused, and no wonder. They'll be asleep now. It's only four in the morning. Timon wanted to come here and stay with you all night, but I said I would. I never sleep much at the best of times, and he was exhausted."

"Matthew?"

"Fast asleep in my bed. Everything's all right, I promise you."

"I gave you the money, didn't I? Or was it a dream. . . . I can't remember. Did I give you the money?"

"Hush, it's all right," Mrs. Carter said gently. "I've already spoken to Mrs. Shaw. We'll send them a check in the morning for the money Matthew borrowed, and she'll forward his luggage to us. He's not going back there. I told her I wouldn't trust her to look after a cat. I never did like that woman. No, Matthew can stay with us until your stepmother has everything fixed. Not in my bed, though. He'll have to share with Timon after tonight."

"Does he know?"

"Yes, we told him. He seemed pleased. Don't worry anymore. You've done enough worrying, my poor girl. Go back to sleep now."

"I suppose you gave him some milk and a slice of fruitcake," Elinor said sleepily, and shut her eyes. Mrs. Carter watched her. After a moment Elinor started turning her head restlessly and murmuring, "The money . . . I don't want . . . I don't know. . . . It's all spilling out on the floor! You can take it! I don't care. Take it. . . . He might have said . . . Why didn't he say?"

"Hush. You're dreaming. It's only a dream."

"Are you the right person?"

"Yes. Yes, my dear. It's all right now," Mrs. Carter said, to calm her. Several times during the night, drifting in and out of dreams, Elinor had been talking, a jumble of words and phrases that had puzzled the old lady. There was nothing about the great gale, the tree falling, or the ceiling coming down. It was about money—and Timon. Several times his name had come up—"Timon won't find it now. . . . I can't, Timon, I can't. I can't give the money back. . . . There'd be nothing . . . nothing. . . ."

Mrs. Carter frowned and sighed. Then, getting wearily to her feet, she went to ask the nurse if she could make herself a cup of tea.

The doctors said Elinor could go home that afternoon. Mild concussion, they said, and shock. Stay in bed for a day or two. Take things easy for the rest of the week. Come back to the outpatient clinic next Monday to have the stitches out of your head—here's your appointment card.

It was Agnes who drove her home. Mrs. Carter had no longer been there when Elinor woke up again. Her curtains were drawn back and the visitor's chair was empty. She was beginning to wonder if she had dreamed that the old woman had sat all night by her bed, and held her hand and soothed her when her dreams were bad.

But then the woman in the next bed had said, "Your grandma's gone home, dear, if that's who you're looking for. She said to tell you Agnes will be coming after lunch, and you're not to worry about anything. How are you feeling, dear?"

Elinor was feeling better. Her head was sore but it was clear inside. She remembered it all, the great wind, the fire they had lit in the cottage, and Timon saying they could stay there, safe and warm. Then the world had collapsed, proving him wrong. There was nowhere safe anymore, Elinor thought. *The money's no good. It'll only bring us bad luck.*

Agnes did not talk much on the way back from the hospital, except to tell Elinor what Mrs. Carter had already told her, that Matthew was to stay with them for the time being.

"He and Timon wanted to come with me to fetch you," she said, "but Timon's taking a day off school and it wouldn't have looked good if any of his teachers had seen him, so—"

She broke off to concentrate on passing a truck, making three nervous attempts before falling back again.

"They always seem to go faster when I try and pass them," she complained. "And this is such a bendy road. I expect it will turn off soon. They usually do if you wait long enough."

"Is there any more news?" Elinor asked, for she felt that she had been away for far longer than just one night.

"I thought I'd leave Mother to tell you. It was her idea to go up to see Mr. Brimly yesterday—"

"Is that where you went? I thought you'd just gone shopping. . . . Was it about Dad? It must have been. Tell me, Aggie, please tell me!"

"It's just that his trial has been fixed for next month. Mr. Brimly says it will only take a short time because he's . . . Mother can explain it better than I can."

"He's going to plead guilty, isn't he?"

"You knew?"

"Janet said that must be why he didn't appeal about the bail. His time in detention will count as part of his sentence, you see, and you get more privileges in detention."

"You all know so much more about everything than I did at your age," Agnes said, sounding as if she thought this was a pity.

"I don't suppose your father went to prison, did he?"

"No. But you mustn't . . . don't think that . . ." The truck in front slowed and turned right. "Now we can go more quickly," Agnes said, abandoning her unfinished sentences with relief.

Timon and Matthew were waiting for them by the gate when they got home, smiling and waving in the washed sunlight, their hair ruffled by a now gentle wind. They ran forward when the car stopped.

"Ellie! Ellie, are you all right? How many stitches did you have? I thought you'd have a big bandage. I thought you'd be done up like the Invisible Man. I don't think much of that dinky little dressing," Matthew cried, hugging her. She'd never known him so excited, so talkative, so obviously pleased to see her.

"Hey, Matt," she said, laughing. "Let me look at you. Oh, your face is all scratched!"

"And my hands, look! That was the holly. I'm a hero. I ran all the way back through the storm to get help, with branches crashing right and left. Timon's a hero too. He carried you for miles—well, hundreds of yards anyway."

"It seemed like miles," Timon said. "There's doughnuts for tea, but you'd better not have any, Ellie. You're much heavier than you look."

They took her into the house, laughing and joking, and settled her on the sofa with two pillows behind her head and a lap robe over her. The little room was more crowded than ever, with Matthew in an armchair and Timon on the floor beside her, and Aggie and her mother busying themselves with the tea. But there were flowers on the table and the mantelpiece. It had a festive air.

"Did Agnes tell you about your father?" Mrs. Carter asked, when they were all settled.

"Yes."

"What about him?" Matthew asked. "She didn't say anything to me."

He listened in silence while Mrs. Carter told him and then shrugged and said, "So he's pleading guilty. We knew he'd done it. We knew all the time."

Agnes said in her soft, breathless voice, "You mustn't think badly of him. He was such a nice boy when we were young, so kind and always laughing. I'm sure he never meant to do anything wrong. He was so much younger than the other directors. They were obviously the ringleaders. It isn't easy to resist people who are older and more experienced than you are."

"Children do it all the time," Mrs. Carter said dryly. "Most children, that is, not you, Agnes. You were always very obedient. However, you're right." She looked across at Elinor. "Don't judge your father too harshly. Though I expect you will, whatever I say. Young people are so stern with their parents. They expect too much of them."

"We don't, do we, Ellie?" Matthew cried.

"I did," she said. "I expected him to let me visit him. I expected him to answer our letters. And when at last he did, I expected him to explain things, not to treat me like a child. But I expected too much. I thought he trusted me, but he didn't. He just made use of me because I was there. And he's turned me into a kind of thief. Why shouldn't I judge him?"

They stared at her in silence, the two women astonished and concerned, only the boys knowing fully what she was talking about.

"You never spent it," Matthew said. "You wouldn't even let me open it."

"We'll have to give it back, Matt. It's no good. We can't keep it. I'm sorry, I thought it would keep us safe, just having it, but . . . we nearly died. You can take it," she said, turning to Mrs. Carter, who looked back in bewilderment. "It's yours. Wait, I'll get it for you."

She got off the sofa, walked out into the passage, and into Mrs. Carter's room. They followed her, asking her questions she didn't bother to answer. The bed Matthew had slept in was unmade and the room smelled of the potpourri the old lady kept in bowls on the windowsill and chest of drawers.

"Don't tell me you hid it in here?" Timon asked, looking at her with respect. "I'd never have guessed that in a hundred years."

"I knew you wouldn't," she said. Lying facedown on the floor, she reached her arm out under the chest of drawers, pushed some flat boxes out of the way, and brought out the small gray suitcase.

"What's that?" Mrs. Carter said, sitting down on the bed and staring. "I've never seen that before. What's it doing in my room?"

"I put it there," Elinor said. "I couldn't think where else to hide it. And anyway, it's yours." She put the case down on the bed beside Mrs. Carter. "It's the money Dad cheated you out of. At least, I think it is. Timon, can I borrow your penknife?"

"What are you doing? You can't force it open!" Agnes cried. "Mother, stop them!"

"No. We'd better see what it is. Go on, Elinor, if that's what you want to do."

Elinor took Timon's penknife and forced open the locks, one by one. Then she flung back the lid of the case.

Chapter Twenty-four

THEY ALL looked down. Then Timon began to laugh. After a moment Matthew joined in, his laughter shrill and a little hysterical. A new white shirt, still in its cellophane wrapping, filled the top of the small case. Elinor snatched it out and threw it on the bed; another shirt followed, pale pink this time, then blue-and-white striped pajamas, all brand new. The two women were laughing now. Elinor did not even smile but went on unpacking the case. Socks, underpants, sponge bag, hairbrush, some sort of band, about four or five inches wide and a yard long, with zipped pockets sewn into it, now empty and flat—

"Let me see that," Mrs. Carter said, taking it from her. She turned it over in her hands, no longer laughing. "A money belt. New by the look of it. Why would he want . . . What's that you've got there? A passport?"

"It's Dad's," Elinor said, handing it over.

They had all stopped laughing now. They watched Elinor in silence as she lifted out the last thing in the case, a fat, buff-colored folder, done up with tape. Ripping away the tape, she emptied it out onto the bed—and there it was, the money her father had stolen.

It was nothing like in her dream. Here was no spreading sea of money flooding over the bed. The banknotes, flat and crisp in their bundles, each done up neatly with a paper band, looked more like a pile of shallow bricks, a modest pile, not nearly enough to make a house for Timon's Ma. Her first feeling was one of disappointment. She'd never wanted her father to be a thief, but like Sophia she felt if he had to be one, he might have done better than this.

"There isn't much here, is there?" she said.

Nobody answered her. They were all gazing silently at the money, their faces solemn, wistful, full of private dreams. Only Agnes's had a look of repulsion, as if the money were some loathsome and infectious disease. When Timon stretched out his hand and picked up one of the bundles, she said quickly, "No! Put it down. Don't touch it, Timon."

"I was only going to count it," he said, looking offended. "There's more than there looks. These are all fifties and there must be . . . let's see . . ." He began to count.

"Put it down, Timon."

He took no notice of Agnes but went on counting, "—forty-eight, forty-nine, fifty. Fifty notes in a bundle. Fifty times fifty is—um—twenty-five hundred pounds. Wow! How many bundles are there? Help me count, Matthew."

Matthew hesitated, glanced at Elinor and then back at the money. "They're not all fifties. Here's a bundle of tens," he said, and his hand reached out in spite of himself.

"Mother, stop them!" Agnes cried. "It's not theirs. It's stolen money. We ought to call the police—"

"No!" Elinor and Matthew and Timon shouted, almost at the same time, so that it sounded like one loud, ragged voice of disapproval.

"What are you thinking of, Agnes?" her mother said. "You're upsetting Elinor with your silly ideas. She's gone very white. I don't think all this excitement is good for her."

"I'm all right," Elinor said. But they insisted that she get into the bed, with the pillow propping her up and the bundles of money spread out before her like sandwiches on a counter.

"Does your head hurt?" Agnes asked contritely. "Would you like an aspirin? Or some camomile tea?"

"No, thank you. I'm fine," Elinor said, though it wasn't true. Her head was sore and she felt dizzy with tiredness. She lay back on the pillows. Someone had drawn the thin green curtains, afraid of watchers in the garden. The room swam in a dim, watery light, as if they were at the bottom of a huge aquarium. Their fingers scuttled over the money like pale crabs.

"How much do you make it, Timon?" Mrs. Carter asked when they had finished.

"Thirty-five thousand, Ma," he said, and somebody sighed.

"It's yours," Elinor cried, pushing the money toward the old lady, wanting to be rid of it. It didn't seem like real money to her. It never had seemed real. It had been something she had to guard, to hold on to, to keep hidden. But now it was over and she was glad. "You have it.

It's not as much as he owes you, but it's better than nothing."

Mrs. Carter sat down on the foot of the bed, looking down at it, arranging it in a neat pile with her freckled hands. "Enough for a flat of my own, with a room for Timon and a garden for Fizz," she said slowly. "Think of it, Agnes. You could have your house all to yourself again. No difficult old mother sleeping in your dining room. A spare room upstairs for your friends to visit. Just think how happy you would be."

"I like having you here, Mother," Agnes said stiffly, "and it isn't your money."

"It is!" Elinor cried. "Dad wanted her to have it. He said so," she lied. "He said, 'Give it back to Mrs. Carter and say I'm sorry.' "

"What a terrible little fibber you are," Mrs. Carter said, laughing. "That doesn't sound like George at all. For one thing, he always called me Aunt Flossie (yes, I know it doesn't suit me). Had you forgotten I'm his aunt? You don't know much about your own family, do you? Not your fault. George never had any time for us. I suppose we are rather a boring lot."

"Dad was always terribly busy," Elinor mumbled, remembering too well the uncomplimentary things her father had said—"A bossy old aunt and a dreary cousin. You wouldn't like them, Ellie."

But she did like them. They were her family, this fierce old lady and poor, kind, put-upon Agnes. And Timon, her foster cousin, if there was such a thing, with his bright eyes and his odd sense of humor. She didn't want to lose any of them.

"He did say something," she insisted. "He whispered

it when he slipped the luggage receipt into my pocket, but I didn't hear what. It might've been that he wanted you to have the money. But I couldn't very well ask him to repeat it with the police there, could I?"

"I suppose not, dear," Agnes said, confused.

"So you see, Mrs. Carter has got a right to it. Dad cheated her out of her savings—"

"Me—and a lot of other people like me," Mrs. Carter said, and sighed. "I'm afraid Agnes is right. It's not really mine. It will have to be shared out among all the creditors—"

"Ma, that's mad!" Timon's voice rose to an anguished yelp. "There're hundreds of them. And all the lawyers wanting their cut. You'd be lucky if you got ten pence each. What good is that to anyone? They wouldn't thank you for it. They'd think you were a fool. At least if you keep it, it'll be doing somebody some good—us. Oh, you're not going to be stubborn, are you, Ma? It's so stupid."

"I know, but what can I do?" she asked. "I've been honest too long, Timon. I can't change at my age."

"I can change at mine, anytime," he said, and snatched a bundle of fifties from the bed.

"Timon! No!" Agnes cried, but he only laughed and held the money out of her reach.

Matthew, his eyes bright with excitement, stretched out his hand toward the bed but Elinor was too quick for him. She grabbed his fingers and squeezed them in her own, hissing in his ear, "Stop it! Do you want to be sent back to Worthing? Do you want to end up like Dad?"

Only Mrs. Carter remained calm, and went on packing the rest of the money back into the folder without a word.

"Damn your eyes, Ma," Timon said, laughing and tossing the bundle to her. "What have you done to me? What's happened to the slick little thief I used to be? If I'm not careful, I'll wake up one of these days with a darn halo on my head. What are you going to do with all that lovely money? Don't give it back to Elinor. She'd only hide it in some crazy place and we'd have all the trouble of finding it again. Besides, she looks better without it. She's lost that mean, suspicious look she used to have, as if she thought we were going to pinch the icing off her cake. She's quite pretty now," he added, which so pleased Elinor that she forgave him the rest.

The two women were talking together, deciding what to do. Elinor was content to leave it to them. She wanted to go to sleep. Perhaps she'd regret what she'd done when she woke up. All that lovely money, as Timon said.

Matthew sat on the bed beside her and whispered, "I don't see why they should have it all. You are an idiot, Ellie. Still, I'm glad we fished you out of the cottage, me and Timon. You haven't thanked us yet, by the way."

"Thank you," she said sleepily, and shut her eyes.

They woke her in time for supper and told her what they had decided. Mr. Brimly was the best person to deal with the money, they said. He would know how to return it. There must be no suggestion that it was an attempted bribe, nor did they want to give the impression that her father had packed a sort of getaway case—

"But he had, hadn't he? He'd put in his passport,"

Elinor said, and could not keep the bitterness out of her voice.

"We don't have to mention that, or the money belt. We don't want to make things worse for your father. Leave it to us, you've done your part, Ellie. Matthew told us about the luggage receipt and how you fetched the case from the station. That was very brave of you. Don't worry, my dear. Nobody can blame you for not giving your own father away. One thing I can't understand is why, when he thought you'd accidentally burned the receipt, he didn't tell Mr. Brimly. He can't have thought it would be still there when he came out. They don't keep unclaimed luggage forever."

"I expect he thought Sophia was lying. She does tell lies sometimes. He probably thought I gave her the receipt, and she was going to take the money and go back to Italy for good. He wouldn't have given her away to the police, whatever she'd done. He loves her terribly, you see."

Agnes was silent. Looking at her, it suddenly occurred to Elinor that perhaps she had loved him, too, ever since they were children together, the boy who'd been kind to her and who was always laughing.

"Do you like your stepmother, Elinor?" Mrs. Carter asked.

"Yes. Yes, I do. You can't help liking Sophia."

"That's just as well," Mrs. Carter said, smiling, "because she's coming back next week. Mr. Brimly told us. That was the second piece of news we had for you. Apparently Sophia phoned him. She said she'd gone back to Italy to see her family and ask them for help. That was sensible of her, more sensible than I would have expected. The young are usually so damn sure that they can manage everything on their own—"

"Mother! Elinor managed very well, I mean, when you think—"

"Who said anything about Elinor?" the old lady said innocently. "I was talking about this Italian girl, Sophia. Her mother summoned all the family and they had a meeting and it turned out that her mother's uncle has a third cousin who owns a chain of cafés over here. He's offered her a job in one in London, with rooms above where you can be all together again. Are you pleased?"

"Yes! Oh yes!" Elinor said, her eyes shining.

"We shall miss you, Ellie," Agnes said a little sadly. "We've liked having you here. Don't forget us, will you?"

"I won't. I'll miss you, too, all of you," Elinor said. "You must come and see us. I don't want to lose you. You're my family."

"London," Timon told her, "isn't so very far away. No need to soak your pillow with tears. You'll be seeing us again. Me especially."

That night Elinor could not get to sleep. She kept seeing again the bleak little gray case, with the pajamas and the money belt and the passport spread out on the bed beside the bundles of money. Where had Dad planned to go? Or had he just acted in a panic, without any plan at all? She didn't know. She wasn't even sure whether he would really have sent for them to join him.

When he comes out of prison, we'll have to get to know him, she thought. We'll have to try and understand.

Chapter Twenty-five

▬▬▬▬▬▬▬

THE CAFÉ was in Hockley, a part of London Elinor did not know at all. Here there were no houses set in leafy gardens, no trees, no tubs of bright flowers; only brick and concrete and glass, litter on the pavement, dust in the air.

"You will not like it," Sophia said gloomily. "How can you like it after your family's house in the country? I know you will not."

"Yes, I will," Elinor said.

She liked it already; the gaudy shops, the cafés, the street markets, and people everywhere, chattering and quarreling and whistling, mothers scolding, children crying and laughing. She preferred their clamor to the nervous birdsong in the dark woods. She was a city girl.

Sophia had met her at Paddington Station, standing on the other side of the barrier, laughing and waving and calling out, "Ellie! Ellie! I am here!" People had looked and smiled, warmed by the sight of her curling red hair and laughing face. All the way on the bus she had chattered and smiled and waved her hands about, so that the one small diamond ring she had kept glittered on her finger like a flying spark. Bambi was well. He had cut another tooth. Her mother's uncle's third cousin's wife, Maria Sancelli, was looking after him this morning—"I did not want to bring him to the station. I wanted both arms free to hug you with," Sophia said.

But when they got off the bus at Hockley and walked through the crowded streets, she became uneasy, and kept looking at Elinor doubtfully.

"You must not expect nice things," she said. "It is not finished. I think it will be a long time. It is not even very clean though I scrub. Yesterday I saw a cockroach," she confessed dolefully. "I step on him but I think he has a family. Who is going to pay good money for cockroaches in their pasta?"

Elinor laughed. The sun was shining and she was determined to be happy. Everything was going to be all right. It must be.

Last week Mrs. Carter had gone up to London on her own to see the lawyer. She handed over the money in the buff-colored folder, with no mention of Elinor or the small suitcase, the passport or the money belt. Her nephew, she'd claimed in a quavery old woman's voice, had left the folder with her some months ago, asking her to hand it over to Mr. Brimly when she went up to London the next day, as it belonged to the company, and he was going to be away for a couple of weeks and would not be able to return it himself. But she'd had an attack of sciatica and had gone to bed, not to London after all. Her daughter had tidied the folder away into a drawer and she'd forgotten all about it.

"My memory isn't what it was," she'd claimed, meet-

ing all the lawyer's questions with a face of elderly inno-
cence. "I don't know. I'm afraid I've forgotten."

There were some advantages in being old, she had
told them gleefully when she got back. Mr. Brimly may
not have believed her story, but he'd given her a receipt
for the money and told her it might help to make a good
impression on the court—especially as George Forest
had already put nearly all of his own money into the
companies in an unsuccessful attempt to save them. It
was unlikely the judge would be hard on him. But, of
course, you could never tell with judges. . . .

Sophia was still talking about the apartment over the
café. "It is big, five rooms and the attic, but there is nothing in them, only the big bed and Bambi's cot and a camp
bed I borrow for you. All our old furniture I sell to pay
bills before I go home. Now we have no curtains, no
carpets, no table. I borrow three chairs from the café, but
if we are busy, I must put them back and we sit on the
floor. Mr. Sancelli give me a little money to buy things,
but not very much, and I am afraid to spend it because
then we have nothing until I get paid."

"It doesn't matter. We like sitting on the floor. And
Timon said he'd come up in the holidays to help us. He's
good with his hands. He made all the cupboards and
shelves in Agnes's kitchen. And Ma said she could let us
have some china. I'm afraid I promised Judy her room
could be pink and white," Elinor said. "But I can do that.
I'll buy the paint." (Judy, far from being overjoyed when
Elinor had told her they could all be together again, had
asked if she could stay with Aunt Cathy. "You should see
my room here, Ellie. It's so pretty, all pink and white. I
don't want to live over a smelly old café," she'd said.)

"I give her the little room, any color she like," Sophia said, and smiled, adding, "I think you like attic all alone better than share with her, no?"

"Much better!" Elinor agreed fervently. "I like attic rooms."

They turned a corner into a short, wide cul-de-sac, and there it was, the Pasta Palace. It was larger than Elinor had expected, with big windows on either side of the entrance, and its name up in neon lights. On the far side was a red front door to the rooms above. Opposite there was a vegetable stand, a hairdresser, and a betting shop with a large picture of a white horse in the window.

Elinor smiled. "We'd better keep Dad out of there," she said. She looked back at the café thoughtfully. "We'll have tubs of flowers either side of our door," she decided. "Ma will let us have some plants from her garden. We'll go around the markets and junk shops. Timon says you can find treasures left out at the curb to be thrown away, that only need a little fixing. We'll all help, Timon and Matthew and Judy and me. We'll scrub and we'll paint. It'll be fun, Sophia, you'll see." She looked up at the windows above the café. "We'll make a palace up there for Dad to come home to," she said.

Snow was lying on the pavement in front of the red door when George Forest came home. Prison had aged him. His face was pasty and lined, and he had put on weight. Elinor and Matthew and Judy had been waiting in the café, their breath clouding the window so that they had to keep wiping it away. When they saw him get out of Mr. Sancelli's car, they came running out, and then hesitated, staring at him as if he were a stranger. He looked back at them and did not say anything.

Then Elinor cried, "Welcome home, Dad," and he strode over and took all three of them into his arms.

About the Author

VIVIEN ALCOCK, a commercial artist as well as a highly successful novelist, has written many books for young readers, including *The Haunting of Cassie Palmer, The Stonewalkers*—a *School Library Journal* Best Book—and *The Monster Garden*, a Carnegie Medal Nominee. *The Trial of Anna Cotman, Ghostly Companions, The Mysterious Mr. Ross, Travelers by Night, The Sylvia Game,* and *The Cuckoo Sister* were all named Junior Library Guild Selections.

Vivien Alcock lives in London with her husband, the writer Leon Garfield.